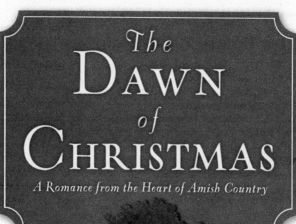

The
DAWN
of
CHRISTMAS

A Romance from the Heart of Amish Country

CINDY
WOODSMALL

WATERBROOK
PRESS

THE DAWN OF CHRISTMAS
PUBLISHED BY WATERBROOK PRESS
12265 Oracle Boulevard, Suite 200
Colorado Springs, Colorado 80921

Hardcover ISBN: 978-0-307-73213-2
eBook ISBN: 978-0-307-73214-9

Previously published as part of *Christmas in Apple Ridge*, copyright © 2012 by Cindy Woodsmall.

Cover design by Mark D. Ford; cover photos: girl, Carie Hill; background, Dale Yoder

Published in the United States by WaterBrook Multnomah, an imprint of the Crown Publishing Group, a division of Random House LLC, New York, a Penguin Random House Company.

WATERBROOK and its deer colophon are registered trademarks of Random House LLC.

Library of Congress Cataloging-in-Publication Data
Woodsmall, Cindy.
   The dawn of Christmas : a romance from the heart of Amish country / Cindy Woodsmall.
      pages cm.
   ISBN 978-0-307-73213-2 (hardback)— ISBN 978-0-307-73214-9
 1. Single people—Fiction. 2. Amish—Fiction. 3. Christmas stories. I. Title.
   PS3623.O678D39 2013
   813'.6—dc23
                                            2013023137

Printed in the United States of America
2013

10 9 8 7 6 5 4 3 2 1

To our dear, lifelong friend Catherine Logan

Your faith is strong and stalwart, yet you understand
the winds of change that sweep through the soul.
You've spent a lifetime going out of your way
to help those who need or seek a transition.
You've tirelessly planted seeds of hope and courage
in every person blessed to come into contact with you,
and since I was a teen, I've considered it a privilege to call you a friend.

As my youth fades a little more each day,
and I see the past with perfect clarity,
I honor your wisdom and counsel and strength even more today.
You own a piece of my heart.

One

Muffled voices drifted through the living room, but Sadie couldn't make out the words. She sat in a ladder back, avoiding Daniel's gaze by staring into a fireplace with its few fading embers. Family members, hers and Daniel's, peered at her with eyes full of pity and shock.

When Daniel had made his intentions known, folks whispered behind her back that little Sadie Yoder had finally snagged someone's attention and she better hold on for dear life. She knew that was true, but she hadn't cared what people thought, not one whit. Daniel Miller had moved to Brim from Tussey Mountain a year earlier, and he'd fallen in love.

With her.

Her, of all people. The one best known for being a quiet stick of a girl who caught no man's eye.

Every day that passed she'd thought her heart might explode from the joy of falling in love. When he'd asked her to marry him, well, she'd all but fainted from the excitement.

Daniel wasn't just any man. He was above her in every way. He was handsome and had a deep voice, strong shoulders, and a way of winning people's respect. At twenty-four, only five years older than she, he already had an established horse-trading business. She'd fully believed in him and felt honored he'd chosen her.

Now...

She lifted her eyes to meet his, and heartbreak stole her breath. If her legs could carry her, she'd get up and walk out.

"Forgive me." Daniel's lips barely moved, his whisper meant for no one but her. He looked as shocked and hurt by his behavior as she was.

She turned her attention back to the stone fireplace. It stood silent, the pile of gray-and-black ashes smoldering from a fire that once burned hot. A perfect depiction of her life.

A blur of crisp magenta folds swirled in front of her, and her cousin Aquilla knelt beside her chair. Aquilla's perfect oval face radiated beauty. Her blond hair framed her head like a halo, and her green eyes were mesmerizing. And all of it was able to steal Daniel's heart before Sadie caught a hint of what was happening.

"Please, Sadie."

Please? What was Aquilla thinking? Did she hope Sadie could also be convinced of her lie? Or did she want Sadie to have the power to erase their betrayal? their indulgence? their sin?

Daniel had been a perfect gentleman with Sadie, but what she'd witnessed less than an hour ago proved he was not unfamiliar with a woman's body. She could still see his hands embracing Aquilla, caressing her in a way that would haunt Sadie for years.

She had invited Aquilla two months ago to come from out of town to help prepare for the wedding. What a fool she'd been.

Aquilla clasped her delicate hands over Sadie's stained ones. "It wasn't as it looked. I promise. You misunderstood."

That was a lie. One Aquilla had already repeated a few times, no doubt hoping it would save her from gossip and from looking like the betrayer she was. Sadie kept her gaze fixed on the fireplace, wishing she could escape like smoke up a chimney. Everyone would leave later, but how many would be unsure of what she'd actually seen? This would be her only chance to defend herself against Aquilla's lies to Daniel's family, but the words begged to stay hidden.

A mere hour earlier Sadie had been making last-minute alterations to her wedding dress. As daylight grew faint, she'd needed a new propane tank for the gas pole light in her bedroom. She hadn't even known Daniel had arrived for a visit. As she'd crossed the backyard, she'd breathed in the fall air and enjoyed the red and yellow leaves of maple and birch trees.

Then she'd opened the shed door. In a moment of time, as quickly as the hope of being loved had come to her, it had fled. Every hope of marrying Daniel shattered. The laughter of their future children silenced.

She'd run back to the house, fleeing a truth she could not escape. Once inside, she'd slammed the door tight, locked it, then fallen against the frame and wept. When she'd looked up, dozens of her relatives and Daniel's were staring at her. She'd forgotten they were there to help prepare for her and Daniel's wedding day.

Daniel and Aquilla had pounded on the door, demanding she let them in.

Sadie's *Daed* had hurried to her, asking what was going on, and she'd whispered what she'd witnessed. The emotions that crossed her Daed's face mirrored her own. He'd been the one to encourage the relationship, nudging the two of them together from the moment Daniel had arrived in the community. When Daed had opened the door to Aquilla and Daniel, Sadie had expected their guilt to be evident on their faces. But they'd looked only upset, and Aquilla's first words were a lie she didn't even stumble over.

Aquilla's eyes had glistened with tears, and her angelic face radiated sincerity. "I fell off a stepladder, and he caught me." She'd turned to face everyone in the room. "She's insecure about Daniel, imagining her worst fears concerning him." She'd wiped tears from her face. "Why would I want the only man she's ever dated when I can date anyone I choose?"

Immediately the heads of loved ones had begun to nod, and murmurs rippled through the room. Daniel had stood by quietly, neither denying nor confirming Aquilla's account. Her cousin had skillfully planted doubt in everyone's mind, and in so doing, Sadie felt what little strength she still possessed drain from her. It wasn't Sadie's nature to defend herself, to stir anger and resentment when the argument would still leave people unsure of who was right.

If given time, would Daniel take up Aquilla's lie too?

Sadie closed her eyes, trying to reconcile what was happening with what was supposed to take place tomorrow. She pulled free of her cousin's hand and rose, hoping her legs would not fail her. Standing mere feet from Daniel, she stared into his eyes, remembering how they'd grown so close over the past months, talking for hours, laughing at things only they shared. She studied him now. Who was this stranger? What did he see when he looked at her? Did his heart break for all he'd forsaken?

He gazed at her. "I swear to you on my life, nothing like this has happened before or ever will again."

She was tempted to believe him. But how could she be sure? Did he mean what he said, or would he say anything to end this nightmare?

She'd never know.

What she did know was that her family believed she'd remain unwed forever if she didn't marry Daniel. Even rebellious teens weren't gawked at or gossiped about like a woman who had never married—at least until the woman was past thirty. Then everyone accepted her fate without further discussion.

Daniel angled his head. "Don't call off the wedding, Sadie," he whispered. "It'll cause a scandal. And there's no sense in trying to weather that."

Visions of him with Aquilla tore at her again. His mouth pressed against Aquilla's, his hands under her dress, roaming over her body. The pain struck again, so deep, so intense, Sadie longed to ease it. She only needed to nod, and he'd embrace her. Relief would rush through him and their families, and everyone would surround her with words of hope and encouragement. Her pain would ease.

But would it ever go away?

She feared not. Doubt would fade when she was in his arms, then grow as bright and scorching as an August sun when she wasn't.

Could she live with that? The seconds ticked by as she studied him, and anger grew in Daniel's eyes.

"Despite what you thought you saw,"—Daniel took a step back, talking loudly enough for most everyone to hear him—"Aquilla has told the truth, and I'm begging you not to call off the wedding over a misunderstanding."

His words hit hard, and she felt the weight of judgment from her family and his bear down on her. Trembling, Sadie struggled to catch her breath. She wasn't strong enough to cope with a broken heart and the fallout of people's disappointment in her if she chose to call off the wedding.

But was she strong enough to marry a liar?

Two

Four years later

S adie rode in the front seat next to the hired driver. Her lips were pressed into a thin line. Summoned. Just like that. She'd been sent for.

She held the letter from her parents, the one they had sent to her boss and trusted advisor. Loyd Farmer had given it to her mere hours ago, his elderly hands trembling in their usual manner.

At least this mandatory family gathering wouldn't be held at her parents' or siblings' homes in Brim. There would be no chance of encountering Daniel.

Thankfully, she hadn't been required to return home but a few times over the years. She could thank her Daed for that. He'd believed her about Daniel's betrayal and had managed to stir up pity for her from the church leaders so they'd leave her alone, allow her to move away, and permit her to go on Mennonite mission trips. Normally, the church leaders would be heavily involved in an incident like the one with Sadie and Daniel and Aquilla. They'd hear all sides and render a verdict. If Sadie had been able to convince the church leaders of what she'd seen, the lovebirds would've been shunned for at least six weeks. But two things stood in her way: an eye for an eye wasn't God's way, and it was her word against Daniel's. Aquilla would have verified Daniel's account of that day. Sadie only had God as her witness. So rather than start a fight she couldn't win, she put the matter in God's hands. Her Daed had appealed to the leaders, telling them that whether Sadie saw Daniel and Aquilla together or simply thought she did, she was broken over her loss. Daed's argument had been convincing enough that they'd let him have final say over Sadie. She respected her Daed for what he'd done, and she owed him a lot, but she liked who she had become because of the extra freedoms she enjoyed. She couldn't give them up now.

Still, her Daed had beckoned her, and in the blink of an eye, she was compelled to head to Apple Ridge, where her mother's family lived. But this wasn't a good weekend to be gone from her job as the floor manager of Farmers' Five-and-Dime. Although they'd probably be fine without her, the Fourth of July weekend was one of their busiest times.

One would think Sadie could get out of bending to her parents' demands by now. With Loyd and Edna Farmer's guidance and support, Sadie had moved into a house in Stone Creek with two Plain Mennonite girls and had gone to work for the Farmers in their variety store.

Sadie had learned that the Stone Creek Mennonite group did mission work at a remote mountain village in Peru. She'd never expected to be able to go with them. It just wasn't done in her community. But her Daed had not opposed her, and what Amish church leader would deny a broken woman the right to serve God by caring for those less fortunate?

None, she'd discovered. Not a one—even if they were not sure what Sadie had seen that day in the shed.

Since her Daed and the church leaders had given her so much leeway for four years, Sadie had expected by now to be free of having to buckle under her parents' wishes. But the opposite seemed to be true. Her Daed had been writing to her more of late and calling her regularly, all with strongly worded pleas for her to return to her Amish roots and live under his roof.

The letter in her hand bore a polite command from her Daed—and he'd sent it to her Mennonite employers. It was a shrewd move on her parents' part. They knew Loyd and Edna would support them and that Sadie wouldn't argue with the elderly couple. And her Daed had chosen neutral ground for what she believed to be the beginning of the latest battle to get her home. She took comfort in the fact that her parents had not pulled the church leaders into their struggle. If they had, she'd have been called home to Brim instead of to her grandmother's place.

The driver pulled onto *Mammi* Lee's driveway. Sadie stared at the old house, dreading what lay ahead of her.

She wasn't the same dedicated-to-the-Amish woman they'd raised her to be, but she couldn't tell them that. All she could do was aim to honor them to the best of her ability and hope her excuse of brokenness from Daniel's betrayal would continue to give her the freedom she needed.

Her *Mamm* came out of Mammi Lee's house, a smile on her face and worry in her eyes. Sadie opened the car door, praying for wisdom and strength to get through the next three days and then return to the life she loved.

She embraced her mother. The warmth radiating from Mamm brought tears to Sadie's eyes. For a moment she wished that circumstances were different. But no, she would return to Stone Creek. The only question was whether she'd do so with peace and love reigning between her and her parents, or if they'd be at war. Of course, there was one other question…

Whether she'd leave as a member in good standing with the Amish or be excommunicated.

Levi stood at the kitchen counter, cracking two eggs simultaneously and dumping the yolks and whites into a bowl.

"How do you always do that?" Tobias stood on his tiptoes, peering into the container.

Levi tossed the shells into the sink, wiped his hands on the kitchen towel tucked into his pants, and passed him the last egg. "Try it."

Tobias smacked the egg against the bowl. Eggshell slid into the bowl while the contents oozed onto the countertop.

Levi chuckled. "Close enough." Running the flat of his hand across the counter, he scraped the mess into the bowl and dug out the pieces of eggshell. He rinsed his hands, dried them, and handed Tobias a fork. "Here, you scramble them."

With twelve eggs in the bowl, Tobias would be busy for a few minutes. In the meantime Levi started a flame under the camp-stove toaster and put four pieces of bread on it.

Tobias gazed up at him, eyes shining. "I love you."

Levi tousled the boy's hair. "You'd better, or no more eggs for you."

How could this sweet boy's mother have left him so suddenly? If Levi could, he'd look her in the eye and demand an answer to that question. For a moment anger stirred, but he tried not to let it pull him under.

The back door slammed. "Do I smell toast?"

Tobias grinned at Levi's brother. "And soon it'll be eggs too!"

Andy came into the room, both eyebrows raised. "Are you ever going to cook that boy anything but eggs?"

"Nope. It's healthy and easy." Levi flipped the bread over, toasting the other side. "Like some smart guy once said, 'If it ain't broke, don't fix it.'"

"No picking on Levi." Tobias grinned. "I don't know anybody that's got an uncle like mine."

"Good answer." Levi loved the kid. He was a pain in the neck at times, but Levi had never seen another like him.

Andy peeled out of his dirty shirt and tossed it toward the doorway of the washroom, then moved to the sink and flicked on the water. "I'll wash up and take over. You still have time to get cleaned up and make it to tonight's singing."

Levi grabbed a plate and put four pieces of toast on it. "Thanks, but I'm not going." Using a potholder, he removed the camp-stove toaster from the flame and set an iron skillet in its place.

Andy scrubbed his hands and arms up to his elbows, washing off caked-on mud. They usually avoided work as much as possible on Sundays, but one of them had to tend to their small herd of horses. "I think Daniel's coming tomorrow, so I took time to get the horse barn in order."

"He's not going to pay us a penny more for those horses because our barn looks good. Still, I'm sure the horses appreciate it, especially since they're spending so much time under the shade trees in this weather." He dumped the raw eggs into the hot skillet, making it sizzle.

"The fine art of sarcasm. Think maybe it's time to give it a rest?" Andy turned off the water and took a dishtowel off the hook.

"Not for a second." Levi stirred the eggs with a wooden spoon.

Andy retrieved three glasses from a cabinet and the milk from the fridge. "You should go tonight."

Levi wrapped a potholder around the handle of the cast-iron skillet and lifted the pan, deciding just how much sarcasm to fling back at his brother. "Are you confusing me with someone who cares what you think?"

Andy grinned. "I'd never do that." He set three plates on the table.

"You do know that's why Mamm brought a stack of clean, well-pressed clothes for you yesterday? She's hoping you'll go tonight. I think it's time you met someone."

Levi dumped the steaming eggs into a bowl and set it on the table. "And I think it's time you minded your own business."

"Tobias, why don't you go to the bathroom and wash your hands?"

Levi wasn't fooled. His brother had just washed up in the kitchen, so there was no reason Tobias couldn't do the same. Andy wanted Tobias out of earshot. The boy scurried down the hall and into the bathroom, slamming the door behind him. His little-boy voice came through the closed door. "Sorry. Didn't mean to do that."

"Not a problem," Andy hollered, then turned to Levi. "Look, we've covered this before. You can't keep avoiding women because I got a bad shake."

A bad shake? Andy's life had been mutilated, and he'd bear the scars in plain sight for the rest of his days.

Levi set the toast and butter on the table. "I understand Mamm and Daed pushing me. But I thought you and I had this resolved."

"I never said it was settled. I left you alone for a while, but you've had enough time."

"Excuse me?" Levi focused on his brother, eyes wide. "Do I live under your roof for *my* sake?"

"No. You do it for mine." Andy snapped at a fly with a kitchen towel. "And I appreciate it. But it's a holiday weekend, and that's when the best singings take place. New girls from the other districts will be here to visit family and meet available men. Go have some fun for a change."

Levi wasn't interested. He'd witnessed one too many women say they were in love, only to walk away later. He was five years younger than

Andy, and he'd spent his childhood shadowing his big brother. If Andy had a good day, Levi did too. So when Andy fell in love and married Eva, Levi felt as if he could lasso the moon. Eva became a sister to Levi, and she'd loved Andy. Levi knew she had. So what caused Eva to break her vows and leave her family?

Something similar had happened to Daniel too. Andy had been in the thick of losing Eva during Daniel's courtship and wedding plans, so Levi was sketchy on the details, but this much he knew: Daniel's fiancée had left him. At least the woman walked out *before* they were married, if only a few hours before. Daniel said she had accused him of being in the arms of another woman, and he admitted he'd been in a room alone with her cousin. But he claimed he never laid a hand on the girl. The last Levi had heard about it, Daniel said his former fiancée had hightailed it somewhere. Maybe Illinois, Peoria, or Peru.

Eva's departure was worse. It'd left Andy without a wife and Tobias without a mother. And they would stay that way since an Amish man could not remarry as long as his former spouse was alive. No exceptions.

"*Kumm* on, Levi." Andy rubbed the center of his forehead. "Please go. I need a break from Mamm's pleading eyes. She's fretting over this. You know she is."

Tobias ran back into the room, holding up his hands to his Daed. Andy pulled a chair out for his son. "You had hands under all that dirt, didn't you?"

The boy nodded and took a seat. "I've been thinking 'bout all these singings everybody keeps telling Uncle Levi to go to. Maybe he doesn't want to go there to meet girls."

"*Ya.*" Levi sat. "I think he's onto something, Andy."

Tobias folded his little hands, preparing for the silent prayer. "Maybe he'd like the idea better if, instead of girls, you'd put a herd of horses in the barn where the singing takes place. He likes them just fine."

Andy looked at Levi, trying not to laugh.

Levi sighed. "Tobias, you got this all wrong. I like girls."

"You do?" Tobias's big brown eyes were filled with innocence.

"I do." Levi turned to his brother. "Fine. I'll go."

Still, he had to figure out a way to settle this issue for his family and his impressionable nephew. But how?

Three

Sadie steadied her breathing. She'd tried to avoid angering her father. After her arrival yesterday, she'd tiptoed through all the conversational land mines, avoiding each potential explosion. Until now.

Daed wagged his finger at her. *"Duh net schwetze."*

She pursed her lips, determined to obey him and not speak—not in English or Pennsylvania Dutch. She ached for the grief she had caused the man who had embraced her so warmly yesterday. The one who had spent a lifetime telling her to listen to God's voice no matter what anyone else said. The one who had understood her need to get away from Brim. There was no doubt that he had a fierce, determined love for her. But now he was angry. And probably afraid. According to him, she had grown up as the sweetest-natured and most obedient daughter. But something in her broke the day she saw Daniel's body entwined with Aquilla's, and there was no going back, not even for her Daed's sake.

Mammi Lee pursed her lips and shook her head. "Sadie."

Her grandmother's voice had never held such sorrow and disappointment. Her family's reaction hurt. So much for being loving and respectful over the long weekend and for not stirring up any arguments. And today was only Sunday.

As soon as she'd arrived, her parents and grandmother had asked her a lot of questions. She'd tried to be honest without giving away her plans to return to Peru with the mission team after Christmas. She figured there would be an opportunity to ease into that conversation closer to December. But while dodging questions about the lease on the home she rented with her friends, her Daed had picked up on her reluctance and pressed her. Before she knew it, she had told everyone about South America. And she was talking about staying there for another year. Maybe two.

Daed focused on her. *"Was iss letz with du?"*

His accusing tone frustrated her. "There's nothing wrong with me. Some of my earliest memories are of you holding my hands while we prayed. You taught me to pay attention to God's leading. That's what I'm trying to do."

He shook his finger at her again. "I told you to be quiet."

"And then you asked me a question." Her voice went up a few decibels. Why was it easier nowadays to live with strangers than visit with her family?

"I've put up with more than enough since you and Daniel parted ways. I've allowed much more freedom than I should have, because I blame myself for having encouraged that relationship. But we both have to accept what happened and start fresh." Daed studied her, then nodded as if answering a question he'd asked himself. "You need to work out your notice at that store and with your roommates. I want you home by Christmas, and I will *not* discuss this again."

Sadie looked across the small kitchen to her mother and grandmother, beseeching them to defend her. Mammi Lee lowered her eyes, but disappointment and hurt clouded her mom's face. Mamm wiped a stray tear, clearly distressed.

Her parents had come all this way to share some time with the Lee side of the family, and even though her mom and grandmother had been cooking all day for a family gathering tonight at an uncle's place, no one would be in a mood to go after this heated argument.

The three stood there, staring at Sadie, wanting her to repent of her dreams. She swallowed hard, trying not to feel broken. "I tried to change the subject and not say anything to upset you. If you don't want to know, please don't make me answer your questions."

"You're our daughter and a baptized member of our community." Mamm pulled a tissue from the hidden pocket of her black apron. "How can we not ask questions?" She wiped her eyes.

"It's time for you to come home." Daed crossed his arms. "A new Amish family has moved to Brim from Ohio. They have seven unmarried sons. Five are of marrying age. If you were home—"

"Daed, stop." Her parents didn't understand her any more than she understood them. All she wanted was to use her faith in Christ on the mission field. Was that so wrong?

Daed rubbed the back of his neck, breaking his stony stare. He turned and went into the next room.

Mamm cleared her throat and pulled a roll of aluminum foil out of a drawer. "Let's line a cardboard box with this and put the food in it." She sidestepped Sadie, speaking to Mammi Lee. "That way, if any of our dishes spill, it won't leak onto our dresses."

Mammi Lee left and returned with a large box. "It may take two this size to pack up all the food."

They acted as if no one had just trampled over Sadie's plans. Why couldn't Mamm see past Daed's fears and think for herself? Why did she have to agree with him every time?

A humid breeze drifted across the room, and the great outdoors called to Sadie. She longed to sneak away, saddle a horse, and ride across fields of green, with no one seeing her but God—an opportunity she didn't have often in Stone Creek.

"Sadie," Daed called.

She went through the tiny *Daadi Haus* and into the living room. He folded the newspaper in his hand and pointed at the couch. She sat and waited.

The balmy air carried the aroma of gardenias, and she could imagine all the wonderful fragrances she'd experience on a long horseback ride.

"I'm sorry I lost my temper. I'll warn you now that I'm losing patience with your stubbornness. And I should." He tapped the newspaper on the arm of the chair. "You've got to stop running. Daniel hurt you deeply, and his lies have only made it worse. I understand that. But it's time to come home and find someone else."

She bit her bottom lip, wanting to correct him. Yes, Daniel had crushed her, and his lies humiliated her, but she'd quit pining over him years ago. What had happened between them had freed her in a way nothing else could. But if she told her Daed that, he'd be more determined that she return home.

His voice droned on and on.

During her three short visits to Brim since leaving, she'd been careful to say little, hoping not to stir up any trouble. She'd never shame her parents or siblings or community by leaving the Order, but she didn't fit easily inside the church anymore. She was best on her own, listening closely for God's voice. He hadn't yet let her down. If He had, she would be married to a lying cheat. So until God gave her direction, she'd do her best to keep the peace with her family.

She took a deep breath and focused on the simple pleasure of being at her grandmother's.

The smell of spices hung in the air, hinting at the promise of tonight's feast at her uncle Jesse's house, less than a mile away. The Amish didn't celebrate the Fourth of July, because doing so would celebrate a war and the killing that comes with war. Still, it was a national holiday, so they often used it as a time to gather with family. Some Amish youth would attend the town's show of fireworks.

"Are you even listening to me?"

Sadie's thoughts jerked back to her father. The honest answer was no, so she shook her head.

He slung the newspaper onto the floor. "Whether three hundred miles from home or on a different continent or in the same room, you make talking with you ridiculously difficult. Which is the way you want it, right?"

"Okay." Mamm walked into the room. "The food is packed up. It's time to go."

Daed stood. "Sadie will stay here. The family will ask her questions, and I don't like any of her answers. It's not a good influence for the younger ones."

Mamm blinked. "After she came all this way to be with the family?"

It was Sadie's turn to be shocked. Mamm never questioned Daed.

Her father tucked in a section of his shirt. "If she had been paying any attention to me, I'd have let her go. But since she's determined to heed only her own thoughts, she won't miss spending time with her cousins."

Daed's judgment was nearly her undoing, but she held her tongue. Without another word he went to the door and held it open while her mom and grandmother toted their baked goods from the house.

Sadie couldn't believe he was leaving her here! She was a twenty-three-year-old woman, not a child. If her father insisted on grounding her from the festivities with her family, she'd be tempted to saddle up Mammi Lee's horse Bay and enjoy a ride. It'd be nice to spend a few hours pretending that nothing owned her except freedom.

Mamm came back into the house and walked over to her. She lingered, looking as if she wanted to divulge a secret.

"I'm fine, Mamm. Go on before Daed gets angry with you too."

Mamm smiled. "He's not as bad as he sounds when he's trying to reason with you. He could complain to the church leaders, and they'd pull you home by your apron strings. But he hasn't. For the last two years he's feared that if we didn't get you home, we'd lose any chance of you returning to your roots."

"I don't want to hurt anyone, and I'll visit when I can, but I don't believe I'm meant to live in Brim."

"You thought you were at one time." Her mother's eyes glistened with unshed tears. "Are you sure it's God's call you hear and not your own?"

Sadie looked out the window, praying for the right words. The emerald leaves on the gardenia bush swayed in the breeze, and a robin disappeared between the thick greenery, probably nesting. Did God want her in Peru, or did she simply long to be as far away as possible from the memory of her greatest pain?

"Sadie?"

She lifted her eyes, hating that tears had begun to well in them. "Can anyone be positive about such a thing?"

Mamm cupped Sadie's face in her hands. "You'd like the Lantz men from Ohio. Two have already found wives." She grinned. "But the one I think would be perfect for you isn't seeing anyone."

"Ya, and how do you know that? Because he says so...like Daniel did?" Taken aback by her own words, Sadie winced. Maybe she wasn't over the pain as much as she'd thought.

"Child." Mamm's singular word was filled with compassion and dismay. She kissed Sadie's forehead. "We'll be home after midnight."

"Give everyone my love." She swallowed hard, unsure if she meant the words or if she was using them as a jab. It was absurd that she wouldn't be at her uncle's home to give them her love.

She flopped onto the couch and stared at the wall. The sunlight faded, and darkness began to deepen. The hands on the mantle clock marked the passing hours. Was everything she longed to do wrong? Or was her Daed overreaching his authority simply because he could? Well, he *could* as long as she honored him by obeying.

The desire to ride swept through her again, but when her Daed had left her behind, he'd intended for her to stay in the house.

A few fireworks popped and crackled in the distance. She sat up and lit a kerosene lantern. The dim yellow glow made a large circle around her. She went to a table and picked up her grandmother's German Bible. A tattered cloth bookmark stuck out of its pages, and she opened it to that spot—Hebrews, chapter 1. She returned to the couch and read, stopping from time to time to think and pray, hoping the words would speak to her.

Four

*L*evi walked from the flaming bonfire in the Stoltzfuses' backyard toward the barn. He'd known the evening would end like this, with him leaving alone while others watched.

"Levi?"

He turned to see Ruth Esh.

Even under the dark sky, her eighteen-year-old face glowed with pink hues, probably because of her forwardness at following him. "I wanted to wish you a happy Fourth."

That's not all she wanted, and he knew it. She'd like him to offer to take her home.

"I hope you enjoy your off day tomorrow, Ruth." He tipped his hat. "G'night."

She continued standing there, brushing off mosquitoes or rubbing spots where she already had been bitten.

He squelched the desire to walk off. "The insects are less likely to bother you if you're near the fire."

"It's barely after nine. Don't you want to stay a little longer? The Stoltzfuses have lawn chairs set up on the back hill facing the town. They said we'll be able to see some fireworks…and afterward maybe you wouldn't mind taking me home."

His horseless carriage stood outside the barn, lined up with two dozen others. But all he wanted to do was leave the rig here and ride home bareback.

Levi admired her courage in asking him right out. "That's really nice of you, but I need to go." He tipped his hat again, hoping she'd walk back to the group. "Evening."

"Bye."

The moment she turned toward the house, he strode for the barn. Once in the dark building, he lit a lantern. Dust floated in the air, easily seen in the soft glow of the lamp. A long row of bridles hung on a dirty plank wall, held up by ten-penny nails. Horses lined the feed trough, grazing on hay while waiting for their owners to return and hitch them to their carriages.

He wanted to bridle Amigo and see what the thoroughbred could really do. Elmer Stoltzfus wouldn't mind if Levi left his rig here and borrowed a bridle. He took one off the wall and walked through the dimly lit barn until he found Amigo. He slid the bit into the horse's mouth.

He led the animal to the lantern, extinguished the flame, then climbed up bareback. He'd take the route where he wouldn't be seen along the way. Maybe he'd stop by the creek and toss a few stones before calling it a night.

When his pocket vibrated, he pulled out his phone. Levi was allowed a cell phone for work purposes, as were others who needed them for business. If he followed the Old Ways, he'd have tucked the phone in a drawer when he got home from delivering a gazebo last Friday night. But he liked being able to text with friends. Amigo's uneven movement made it a little challenging to read the message, but he saw enough to know his younger cousin was harassing him about leaving the singing alone…again. If Matthew had any sense, he wouldn't be engaged at nineteen years old to a girl who was seventeen. They couldn't possibly know themselves well enough to make a lifetime promise.

Levi had been given a gift: insight into the gamble involved with loving a woman. No wonder the apostle Paul said that if a man could stay single without sinning against God, he should do so. His family had witnessed firsthand that women were not worth the risk. So why did they always press Levi on the subject?

Frustration circled, and Levi gripped the phone as if wanting to squeeze the life out of it. He clutched the reins and urged the horse to go faster and faster. The muggy night air felt cool against his skin. After a few moments several loud booms rang out. *Fireworks.*

Without warning, the horse reared up on his two back legs, whinnying, and the phone flew out of Levi's hand.

"Whoa!" He tugged on the reins, trying to bring the animal under control, but the air vibrated with another round of fireworks. Amigo reared and kicked higher and faster.

"Easy, boy." Levi's voice wavered like Jell-O being shaken, and Amigo bucked harder. The darkness around Levi blurred, and when the horse began to spin, Levi was no longer sure where the road lay and where the patch of woods was. Amigo came to a sudden stop, and Levi sailed over the horse's head.

He landed with a horrid thud. Pain shot through every inch of him, and he couldn't catch his breath. He tried to relax, hoping that he just had the air knocked out of him.

God, please.

His breath returned with a vengeance, and he sucked in heavy air. But pain ricocheted through his back, and dread surrounded him even more than the darkness of night. He needed help, but he could feel consciousness slipping away. Was he going to die here, a place where no one was likely to find him until Old Man Hostetler decided to cut his hay again...sometime next spring?

It hurt to breathe. A sharp pain skittered up and down his torso and to the top of his head. He felt as if he were rolling on shards of glass. But he couldn't move.

He needed help, and he could get it...if he could get to his phone.

Anxiety grew like a shadow from the ground and stood over him, looming all around as if it were strong enough to snatch his life right out of him.

Levi pried his eyes open, almost startled when he didn't see a menacing Grim Reaper above him, poised to strike. The black sky reminded him how sinister the world felt at times, but then the stars looked like white marbles that he could hold in the palm of his hand.

If he lived through this night, he'd look back on this moment and recall seeing the universe in all its majesty and recognizing he was only a powerless man staring into the vastness of an all-powerful God.

The sounds of night faded as he slipped into darkness.

Jonah eased into the bedroom, a cup of hot tea in hand.

Beth opened her eyes for a moment. "I'm awake." His wife sat upright, holding her head.

Jonah adjusted the pillows. She sank against them and then held out her hands for the mug.

With her eyes closed, she took a sip. "As soon as my head stops spinning, I'll be fine."

He sat in the chair beside her, admiring her beauty even after such a hard few days.

She blinked and then focused on him. "Oh, honey, stop looking so sad. It had to happen. We were both perfectly healthy for a year leading up to the wedding, and we've had seven months of wedded bliss without so much as a cold, even through the long winter months of serving hundreds of customers. So it's no wonder you picked up a stomach flu and shared it with me. I'll be fine by tomorrow."

"I was better in twenty-four hours. You're going on three days."

"My goal is to have these symptoms linger until you feel so guilty you'll never share another virus with me."

"You accomplished complete dishonor on my part the first minute you turned pale."

She chuckled.

He loved her laugh. Her voice. Her heart. Her tenacity and stubbornness and exuberance and…

Jonah took her hand in his and kissed the back of it. She had no idea what she did to him, and his desire to take care of her, to protect her from all harm grew stronger every day. But a man could not share these feelings with a woman like Beth. She didn't want to be taken care of. She wanted to make strong decisions and carry them out. And that's what she did and had been doing since long before they met.

Still, this illness concerned him. He cleared his throat. "I want you to be seen tomorrow."

"I'll be seen. I'll wake up feeling better, and customers will see me all day."

"Beth, don't be difficult. You know what I mean." He'd feel better once she saw the doctor. Doctors who tended only to the Plain community set up their clinics to be a one-stop answer. Otherwise the multitude of uninsured Amish and Mennonites wouldn't go. So whether a patient needed a severed digit sewn back on or a cancer screening or an x-ray, Dr. Baxter took care of it at his office.

Beth crossed her arms, a slight pout on her lips. "We've been advertising tomorrow's specials since Memorial Day."

"And I'll see to it the store runs smoothly." He kissed her hand again.

"Lizzy's off on another trip with Omar. You'll need me."

Beth's aunt had married the bishop, so the two of them traveled regularly to visit the other church districts where Bishop Omar would be the guest preacher. It was all part of being a bishop. But since the wedding, Lizzy traveled more weeks than she was home.

Jonah squeezed her hand. "I'm sure I'll miss you being at the store, but I'll be fine, and most of the hired girls will be there to help too."

"It's the Fourth. The doctor's office isn't likely to be open."

"Dr. Baxter takes off about five weekdays a year, and the Fourth isn't one of them."

"Wonderful." Her playful frustration rang clear. "Are all doctors whose practice is limited to Amish and Mennonite communities that steadfast?"

"I don't know, but I'd appreciate if you'd stop trying to change the subject as well as my mind." He paused. "Please."

She sighed. "Husbands."

She whispered the word in mock disgust whenever he annoyed her. But her response let him know he'd won. This time.

Usually winning brought him a sense of amusement or playful victory, but the fact she'd given in as easily as she did only added to his concern.

Five

With the old Bible in her lap, Sadie prayed. But the more she did, the more she felt an overwhelming desire to ride Bay. How could she crave going against her father's wishes while praying for wisdom? That made no sense at all.

She closed the Bible. Was she so rebellious that she couldn't do as her Daed wanted for one evening?

She ran her fingertips across the worn leather of the Bible. *God, what is wrong with me?*

The desire to saddle Bay tugged at her even stronger. Apparently she *was* too rebellious to do as her Daed wanted. She sighed and took the lantern into her bedroom. She lifted her overnight bag onto the bed and pulled out her riding clothes. Once dressed, she removed her prayer *Kapp* and untwined her hair. After running her fingers through the waves, she created a long but loosely woven french braid. If she was going to ride Bay over unfamiliar terrain, especially at night, she had to wear pants. And she couldn't wear a prayer Kapp or have her hair pinned up. Her head would look Amish while the rest of her looked *Englisch*. If anyone saw someone riding who looked Amish, it could be traced back to her, and the news would bring shame to her father and trouble to herself. But if people spotted a girl riding who they thought was Englisch, no one would think anything about it.

She carried the lantern with her and left the house. A muggy breeze stirred the lush trees, and fireworks popped in the distance. The clear sky above carried a few white, shining jewels despite the summer haze.

Sadie opened the barn door, and the old mare raised her head. Bay wasn't particularly fast, but Sadie believed the horse loved their rare long nights of riding as much as she did.

When Sadie had Bay ready to leave her stall, she blew out the lantern and mounted the mare. The *clip-clop* of hoofs against the ground made Sadie's heart pick up its pace. She went slowly at first, giving Bay time to warm up. Once they were on the path that led to a stranger's pasture, Sadie loosened the reins, allowing Bay to pick up speed. The mare gave it her all, and Sadie intertwined her fingers through the mane to hold on over the rough landscape.

The sights and smells of summer in Apple Ridge revived her weary soul. Living in Stone Creek, a town of considerable size, had a very different feel to it. An occasional firework went off around her, but the loudest of them had ended before she began her ride.

The moon sparkled off the water in the brook as Bay trotted across the shallow creek bed. Sadie patted the mare's neck. "Good girl. We rode with the wind, ya?"

Bay continued onward, but an odd sound arose from the ground. Sadie tensed. She clicked her tongue, ready to nudge her heels into Bay's side and move back toward home, but then... Which direction *was* home? She tugged on the reins, slowing Bay while she searched their surroundings for a familiar landmark. How far was she from Mammi Lee's? Ten miles? Maybe fifteen?

Another groan made her skin crawl, and she studied the ground. Bay's hoofs shifted and trod the thick grass, leaving clear imprints.

The moon's glow revealed other horse tracks, and Sadie feared it was time to bolt from the area. But she directed Bay to follow the beaten path. The tracks continued for a short distance, then made a circle and went back in the same direction.

On the horizon she saw a shadowy figure. Was that an animal? Yes, it might even be a bridled horse standing at the edge of the field near a patch of woods. Although her curiosity was piqued, she wasn't about to go near that area to check it out. With fear rising, she nudged Bay into a gallop toward the creek.

Once there, Sadie risked a glance behind her. She didn't consider herself a coward. How many women went out by themselves at night for the sheer joy of it? Yet here she was, running home simply because she'd heard a groan in the darkness and seen something that looked like a bridled horse in silhouette.

Unable to shake free of her fear and yet chiding herself for being so skittish, she clicked her tongue and tugged on the right rein until Bay headed back toward the sound.

"Hello?" She peered into the woods, watching for any sign of life. Other than the animal she'd seen earlier—whether cow, deer, or horse—she saw no movement.

As she neared the creature, it whinnied and backed up. Definitely a horse. Reins dangled from the bit to the ground, but it wasn't tethered to anything.

She dismounted. *"Begreiflich." Easy.*

She made several attempts to get closer, but the horse kept backing away. *"Gut Gaul.* Kumm." The horse calmed a bit, ears perked to listen to Sadie's low voice. When Sadie drew close, she took hold of a dangling rein to keep the animal from running off.

"Begreiflich," she repeated softly as she ran her hand down the horse's leg. She didn't feel any broken bones. "Where's your rider?"

Peering into the woods, she looked for any sign of another person, a moving shadow or something. When she saw nothing out of the ordinary, she looked across the field. The grass stood at least a foot tall, high and thick enough to conceal a body. She didn't like the idea of hunting for someone, but even so, she tethered the stray horse to a low-hanging branch, mounted Bay, and followed the tracks in the grass.

She moved slowly, searching the area. Just beyond where the tracks ended, she saw a shadowy lump in the grass. She nudged the horse forward, one step at a time. The desire to flee overwhelmed her, but she paused a few feet from the mass, studying it through the darkness.

A man.

She got off her horse and crouched, realizing the man wore Amish clothing.

"Hello?" She patted his face, but he remained motionless. "Hello? Can you hear me?" She spoke in clear English, hoping not to reveal her Amish accent. If word of how she was dressed leaked back to Mammi Lee's community, her Daed's patience with her would go from thin to nonexistent.

How can you think about yourself right now?

She had to get help. Where had she seen the last house—two, maybe three miles back? Looking across the land, she realized afresh how turned around she was.

"Can you hear me?" When he didn't budge, she pressed two fingers against his neck. His pulse met her fingertips, and relief exploded in her, feeling much like fireworks themselves. "Please wake up."

Regardless of his being Amish, she patted his pants pockets, hoping he had a phone. He didn't, and she again checked his pulse.

His face turned toward her, and she lowered his jaw as if responding to her touch. He moaned, startling her.

Excitement suddenly soared in her, and she was tempted to double her fists and jab them into the air. Instead, she placed a hand on his cheek and rubbed her thumb across it.

"Stay calm and try not to move. I need to get help."

She studied her surroundings. A silhouette of massive trees was in the distance, a dirt road lay a few hundred feet away, and a fence line stood to the west. But where was the closest house?

He raised a hand toward her. "Please…"

He said something more, but she couldn't hear him. She lowered her ear to his mouth.

"If you can help me get up…"

She started to put her hand in his, but something about it didn't feel right, and she lowered her hand. "Not yet."

"Please."

"Stay still." She took his hand in hers, and he clutched it firmly as she lowered it to his side, allowing him to hold it. "We're doing this my way."

His eyes opened, staring at her with disbelief. Then his eyes closed, and his hand released its grip on hers.

She patted his face. "Hello?" Nothing. Now what? While trying to think what to do, she saw his fingers moving. "Hello?" She slapped his face a little harder.

"My…" The whispered word trailed off.

"Do you know where we are?" She lowered her ear to his mouth again.

"Phone."

"You have a phone?"

He didn't respond to her, and she got on her hands and knees, patting the ground around him.

Nothing.

A lot of unmarried Amish men and women carried cell phones. They weren't forbidden from doing so until they joined the church, but even then more and more of the younger generation kept them close.

She fumbled through the tall grass. "God, my most trusted friend, please, You know where his phone is. Help me, please." With the darkness of the night and the height and thickness of the grass, she could be within a hair of putting her hand on it and never see it.

Then a buzzing sound came from nowhere, and she focused all her senses on it. She followed the noise, going one direction and then another. She panicked. What if it stopped before she could find it? She listened intently. *Please, God…*

There! That's where the sound was coming from! She hurried, thrilled as the buzz grew louder. She spotted a blue glow in the grass and ran toward it. After snatching the phone from the thick growth, she dialed 911 and then ran back to the man.

After a few rings a female voice said something she couldn't make out.

"There's a man down in a field." Sadie knelt and nudged the man, hoping for another response, but he didn't budge. "I think he was thrown from a horse."

"Is he conscious?"

"He was for a few moments but not now."

"Is he breathing?"

She knelt beside him and pressed her fingers on his neck again. "He has a pulse."

"Is he bleeding?"

Sadie checked the ground around him. "I don't think so."

"What's your location?"

"I…I don't know. I'm somewhere in Apple Ridge, Pennsylvania."

"Is there a street sign near you?"

"I'm in the middle of a field. There's a road a few hundred feet away, but there's no intersection with a street sign for miles. I'd have to ride my horse to find out." She started to get up, but the man moaned.

Sadie's heart pounded. "When he woke, he asked me to help him get up. If he would wake up again, I could get him on a horse and get him to his family, a place with a known add—"

"Ma'am, *do not move him!* Don't move any part of him. If he begins to stir, you need to keep him still. Do you understand?"

"I understand." But what if he awoke and wanted to get up? How was Sadie supposed to make this man obey her?

"If he wakes, try to keep him conscious, and do what you can to keep him warm. But he must remain lying exactly where he is. Can you check his pockets for identification without moving him?"

What difference does it make who he is? Cupping the phone between her chin and her shoulder, she did as the woman asked, but there was no sign of a wallet. She hovered over his face. "Hello?"

His breathing altered, and the fingers on one hand moved.

"Do you know where we are?"

He seemed to reach for something. She put her hand in his, and he tightened his fingers as if needing reassurance that someone was here. She used her free hand to touch his face, hoping to coax him to respond. "It's okay. I've got help on the line. Do you know where we are?"

He stirred, even opened his mouth, but she could hear no words.

She moved her ear closer to his face again.

"Zook…Road. Three miles…north of…Cherry Hill…intersection."

Tears welled in Sadie's eyes. "Excellent!" She caressed his face as she reported this to the operator. The woman on the other end of the line repeated it back to her.

"Yes. That's right."

The woman didn't respond.

"Hello?"

Nothing.

"Hello?"

Sadie looked at the phone. No lights were on. She punched several buttons but heard no sound of any kind.

The man raised a hand.

She clutched it and lowered it to his side. "Stay still, please."

He shivered, and she frowned. It was hot and muggy, but he breathed and trembled as if he were freezing. Sadie went to her horse, removed Bay's saddle, and plunked it to the ground. She grabbed the blanket and unfolded it while walking back to him. After covering him with it and tucking it around him as best she could, she sat beside him.

"Help's on the way." Since his arms were under the blanket and he responded well to touch, she stroked his cheek. Thank heaven, his shaking had eased.

Under the glow of the moon, she saw him close his eyes. His body went limp. She jabbed her fingers into his neck, feeling a faint rhythm. "Hey! Wake up!" She screamed in his face. "Can you hear me?"

But he didn't budge, and his pulse seemed to fade.

Six

A female voice commanded Levi to wake up. He pried his eyes open.

The outline of a woman hovered over him. She held a cell phone in one hand. Did angels wear jeans and boots and carry a phone?

She seemed perturbed with the phone as she kept pressing numbers. He tried to speak but only managed a moan.

She crouched beside him. "Stay still. Completely still. Okay?"

He wanted to get his hand free of the blanket, but when he tried, she lowered the cover and firmly intertwined her fingers with his. "It's okay. Help is on the way."

"You're no angel."

She laughed. "I'm afraid my father would agree with you completely, especially if he arrives at my grandmother's place to discover I'm not there."

"He'll be worried."

"No. He'll know I've gone riding. He'll just be angry." She released his hand and eased his arm to his side. "What's your name?"

His head pounded. He had to concentrate to answer her. "Levi."

"I'm Sadie." She sat down next to him.

"Amigo...my horse... Is he hurt?"

"He's spooked but appears fine. I think he needs a name change, however, because that horse is no friend of yours."

Her sense of playfulness brought him some much-needed relief. He mustered his strength to talk. "I can't. I have no idea what the Spanish word is for 'enemy.'"

"Believe it or not, it's *enemigo.*"

"You're making that up."

"One might think that, but I promise it's true." She shifted. "Do you live around here?"

"On Hertzler Drive."

"Is that near Hertzlers' Dry Goods?"

His head throbbed, and he closed his eyes.

"Levi, look at me."

He tried but couldn't find the strength. Her hands cradled his face.

"Levi," she sang his name. "Open your eyes." She paused. "Levi, *now!*"

A sensation of being pulled from the bottom of a pond tugged him awake. "It's not nice to yell at people you just met."

"If you don't open those eyes, I'm going to slap someone I just met."

It wasn't easy, but he made himself look at her.

"Good." She smiled. "I was asking where you live."

"A mile or so from the dry goods store."

"I've been to that store with Mammi."

His head spun. He'd never been so befuddled, but did she use the word *Mammi*? "You have Amish family?"

She hesitated. "Sort of." She stood. "I need to get something. Stay very still."

"You're leaving me?"

"I may hurt you if you close your eyes, but I'm not leaving." Then she disappeared.

She *sort of* had Amish family? Did that mean some of her family was once Amish but no longer?

She returned with a saddle, which she put near his shoulder. When she sat, she propped her elbow on it and leaned her head on her hand. "I'm just getting comfortable. I imagine, with the holiday, ambulance services are very busy. One might not show up for a while."

Pain shot through him, and he moaned despite his resolve. His breath came in short, catching spurts. "Sorry. My left leg hurts."

"Try not to think about it."

He glanced up at her, studying her features. "Great plan."

She chuckled. "Got a better one?"

"No."

"Since we're strangers, how about if we play twenty questions?"

He took short breaths. "I already asked one. You didn't answer."

She propped her knuckles over her mouth, watching him. "The question game is a good one—short, back and forth, only discussing things each of us is interested in. But before I began my ride tonight, I was careful so no one could connect me to my relatives in Apple Ridge, and if I answer you, I would place in your hands the power to change my life. I won't give that to anyone."

That was a telling statement. Did she mean it? "Not anyone? Ever? Not even the man you love?"

"Especially not him."

Despite his pain, an eerie sensation swept over him. "I'm not really awake, am I?"

She leaned close, peering into his eyes. "Levi?"

The warmth of her hand against his cheek seemed real, but he had to be dreaming. Catching a glimpse of her heart was like seeing into his own—filled with distrust and determination to steer life onto the safest path possible. Maybe this was God's way of talking to him. He was convinced the world was too big for this kind of coincidence. For him to be thrown from his horse, land on his back in the middle of nowhere, then be found by a woman whose thinking was so close to his own?

This was no coincidence.

Well, real or dream, he needed her to tell him more. "After what you're doing for me, do you think I'd betray your confidence?"

"Probably not, unless it profited you in some way, through money, pleasure, or maybe just ego."

He closed his eyes, trying to block out the pain. "I think you've got me beat."

"How so?"

"I thought *I* was distrusting of the opposite gender. You're way beyond distrust and square in the middle of intolerance. Why?"

She started to pull her hand away. He reached for it and then howled in pain from the movement. "If we wrestle, I'll lose."

She held his hand and eased it to his chest. "Then let's not. I'd hate to have to live with the guilt of having beat up someone I was trying to help."

"I appreciate that."

"Do you have someone special, Levi?"

"Do this often, do you? Find broken men sprawled in a dark field and ask them out? I'm in no mood for a date, but thanks."

She laughed, and the sound echoed against the night, easing his concern that she wasn't real.

He drummed his fingers on his chest, feeling more clearheaded.

Except for his leg, his pain was subsiding. "Much to my family's horror, I'm seeing no one."

"Boy, do I understand that. I didn't think parents were as hard on guys about that."

"You haven't met my brother. He's the worst."

"Okay, twenty questions, but past loves are off-limits."

She must have been in love at least once. He'd like to ask her about it, to understand what it felt like, what the big pull to find someone was really about.

He drew a sharp breath as pain throbbed through his leg and lower back.

She tucked the blanket around him and took his hand in hers again. "I'm Amish, and so is my family. But that's not how we're going to play this game. I'll ask a question, and I'll have twenty tries to get the right answer. You simply say yes or no. Whoever asks the fewest questions before coming up with the right answer wins. My turn. What color are your eyes?"

"That's hardly fair. There are only a few choices of eye color."

"Brown?"

"Someone give the lady a cigar."

"No thanks. I gave them up last week."

"My turn to guess yours. Brown?"

"Nope."

"Blue?"

"Nope."

"Green?"

"Nope."

"Okay, you're just lying to me."

"I'm not." Sadie giggled.

"I'm injured, and you're fibbing to win the game."

"They're hazel."

"Isn't that a shade of brown?"

"Technically I think it is. But if I wear green, my eyes look green. If I wear blue, they look gray."

"So what color do they look when you wear purple polka dots?"

"I told you, I'm as Amish as you are. There is no wearing of polka dots. Did you fall off your horse or something?"

He liked her spunk and how she said things dryly when teasing. "I hope we're here when the sun comes up, because I want to see your weird eyes."

"Do you want my entire family, including Mammi Lee, to turn my future inside out just so you can look into my eyes?"

"Well, since you put it that way...yes." He smiled as she chuckled. "I know a few Mammi Lees in the area."

"No shortage of Lees in this neck of the woods."

"You know someone Amish who has a unique name?"

She chuckled again. "You can choose any combination of names, and I bet you and I both know at least ten people with the same name."

"Which Mammi Lee is yours?"

"Verna Lee. Her husband was a woodworker who once made toys for Hertzlers'."

"I know Verna. We don't live in the same church district, so I haven't seen her in years. But my older brother apprenticed under your grandfather, and I went with him a time or two when I was around fifteen. One time she received a package from you. She loved her little Sadie, the girl who made soaps and candles and sent them to her."

"One of Verna Lee's grandchildren. Number four thousand five hundred and eighty-two, I think."

He chuckled.

Fireworks boomed in the distance, and Sadie jolted. "It's okay," he said. "I'll keep you safe."

"Uh-huh." Her playful tone mocked him.

Without moving his head, he could see multicolored flashes of light in the sky behind Sadie. "Look."

She turned. "Beautiful."

If the fireworks weren't exploding in the sky within his direct gaze, he wouldn't be able to see them. Of course, they could see only a portion of the light display. She moved to his other side so she could see them and face him. They watched in silence for a little while.

She patted the blanket, probably to make sure it was keeping him warm. "Does your brother make toys?"

"He did. I took over."

Her eyes grew large, and for once he didn't feel self-conscious for admitting he made toys. It wasn't his only business, but he enjoyed doing it. Their conversation kept a steady pace, and they stopped talking in English. It surprised him how much they could talk about and how interesting he found each topic. It'd come naturally to tell her he lived with his brother and nephew, but he'd stopped short of saying anything about his missing sister-in-law. Thankfully, either Sadie hadn't noticed, or she was too polite to ask. They even talked about where she lived and her need to earn money to return to the mission field. He was so caught up in their conversation, he didn't notice when the fireworks ended.

She tilted her head and sat up. "I hear a siren. It's probably the ambulance. I'd better move to the road so I can flag them down." She stood, brushing off her clothes. "I need to get back to Mammi's as soon as you're in the ambulance. Is there someone I can call for you?"

"You can find my brother's phone number in your Mammi's Amish directory. It's Andy Fisher on Hertzler Drive."

"You stay still. Okay?"

"*Denki,* Sadie."

She smiled. "You're most welcome, Levi."

She hurried toward the road, and Levi wondered if he'd ever see her again. As odd as it seemed, he hoped he would.

Seven

B eth fidgeted with her patient gown as she sat across from the doctor. Her heart was racing.

Pregnant?

She had missed a couple of cycles, but that wasn't unusual.

Pregnant? By the time she and Jonah had married, they were a decade older than most Amish newlyweds. They'd discussed children before they married, and their conclusion was to be grateful and content to have each other. Their well-meaning relatives on both sides of the family had said that because of their ages, it could take them longer to conceive than most Amish newlyweds. So she and Jonah had agreed not to put pressure on themselves about having babies.

Jonah had stronger opinions about conceiving than she did. He suggested they ignore the possibility, not think or talk about it for at least two years. After they were married, she'd found it very comforting to know he wasn't quietly pacing the floors, needing her to come up pregnant before he could feel satisfied or complete. Now, a mere seven months later, they were expecting.

"You're sure?" Beth tried to steady her voice.

He chuckled. "My practice is among the Amish, and whenever a married woman comes in with any flu-type symptoms, we run a blood test to check for pregnancy."

Beth ran her hand over her flat stomach. Jonah would be beyond thrilled. Excitement skittered through her.

The doctor stood. "Since you're unsure of your last cycle, I'd like to do a sonogram."

She nodded. He helped her lie back on the table. A nurse came in, and within a minute Beth saw a tiny, shadowy image on the monitor. Tears trailed down her face as the baby's heartbeat pulsed fast and loud. This tiny being had a heartbeat! Their child had been growing inside her, and she hadn't even realized it.

The realization of life's many gifts lingered in front of her, and she couldn't help but admire them. How had she gone from being a lonely woman wearing all black to being married to someone as perfect for her as Jonah? And now they were expecting their first child!

The doctor angled the wand one way and then another. Each time, he tapped some keys on the keyboard, and then green lines showed up on the monitor. "According to the measurements, I'd say you're about eleven weeks along. Most women feel a surge of nausea at around eight weeks."

"Food has tasted funny, and I haven't been very hungry. I remember feeling sleepy at the oddest times for a while, but I thought it was because the store's been busier than usual since we added larger-ticket items to our inventory."

He put the wand on the cart, and the nurse cleaned the gooey stuff off Beth's stomach.

"We'll let you get dressed, and then I'll be back to talk."

Both the nurse and the doctor left the room. She felt…invincible, as if the fear and death and sadness of the world couldn't erase the joys she and Jonah would have raising this child. Tears welled again. Once dressed, she sat in a chair and poured out thanks to God for this gift.

There was a knock on the door, and the doctor came in. He asked questions, answered the ones she could think up at the moment, gave her papers and pamphlets and loads of instructions and a prescription for vitamins. She couldn't wait to tell Jonah.

As hard as it was to keep secrets from her driver, Beth didn't say anything to her about being pregnant. Gloria had been her driver since Beth was eighteen, but Jonah had to be the first to hear Beth's news. When Gloria parked in front of the store, Beth hurried inside.

She made sure her expression was normal. Numerous employees said hello when she entered. She spoke to each while looking around the store for her husband. Finally she spotted him stocking candles.

As soon as he saw her, he asked, "How are you feeling?"

"Better."

He smiled, a sense of calm radiating from him. "Gut."

"But I didn't need a doctor because of a virus. By the time I arrived at his office, I was over it."

"It's still good you went."

"True." She took him by the hand, and without asking any questions, he followed her into the office and closed the door. They shared lunches here and talked about business, but most of all, this was where they went when they needed to talk…or steal a few kisses.

When they were courting, after their engagement but before he moved to Apple Ridge, she'd sit in the office and talk to him on the phone for hours.

Now she sat on the front edge of the desk. They were about to share the greatest gift yet with each other.

"What's on your mind, sweetheart?"

"I have news. Good news." She took his hand and put it over her stomach. "I heard our child's heartbeat today."

Jonah's brows tightened, as if he feared he'd heard her wrong. "You're pregnant?"

"Due the third week in January."

Jonah hollered and picked her up. She giggled. "Shh. Everyone must have heard you."

He set her down and jerked open the door. Several people were staring at the office.

"It's okay, folks. I just heard good news concerning the arrival of an important item." He closed the door. "They're fine now."

She laughed.

He hugged her tight. "I never imagined being so happy."

"Me either." Her lips met his, and she relished the moment.

The phone rang. She had to answer it. If she didn't, one of the girls would come into the office to get it. Beth picked up the receiver. "Hertzlers' Dry Goods."

A woman's voice said, "Beth, is that you?"

"Yes, it is. How may I help you?"

"It's Priscilla." Beth couldn't recall the last time Levi's mother had phoned the store. "Levi won't be able to keep his appointment with you today."

Beth flipped open her calendar, realizing Levi should have been at the store two hours ago. She wouldn't have been here, but Jonah would have made time for Levi. "That's fine, Priscilla. Does he want to reschedule for tomorrow?"

Priscilla explained what the last sixteen hours had been like for Levi. Beth's nausea returned, and when her eyes met Jonah's, he moved in closer.

"Levi has a mild concussion, a tiny fracture in his neck, and a broken leg."

While Beth's day had been one of exciting news, the Fishers' day had been one of turmoil. She let Priscilla tell her everything, and then they said their good-byes.

Jonah leaned against the desk. "Will he be okay?"

"Apparently so. His horse threw him. According to Priscilla, a doctor told him it's a good thing he didn't try to get up. Seems a lot of people ignore this kind of injury until it paralyzes them down the road. A woman found him and called for an ambulance. He's not even home yet. The hospital hasn't released him, but his family expects him in a few hours."

"One of us needs to go see him. I can't get away tonight. I have a shipment arriving after hours. Maybe Mattie could go with you."

"Ya, sure." Beth sighed. "Sometimes it seems there are too many accidents among our people."

"A lot of it is how we live—as rugged in some ways as our pioneer ancestors." Jonah put his finger under her chin. "Speaking of safety, I want you to make an appointment with the midwife. When she says it's time, you keep a cell phone with you so you can reach her. You don't balk. Okay?"

Beth grinned and moved into his arms. "Since you know exactly how you want this pregnancy to be handled, maybe you should be carrying the baby."

Jonah pursed his lips. "God knows what He's doing. You carry the baby, and I'll save my strength to carry or drag you as needed."

She chuckled. "Are you saying I'm stubborn?"

"No way I would say such a thing"—he kissed her—"out loud to my expectant wife."

Eight

With Levi and last night still fresh in her mind, Sadie put her bag into the car, said an awkward good-bye to her parents, and got into the vehicle.

Whitney put the car in reverse. "Did you have a nice visit?"

"It had some interesting moments."

Like meeting a stranger who saw life as she did. She'd like to know how Levi was doing. She'd used the phone in Mammi Lee's shanty last night to call Levi's brother. The phone had rung for a while before a groggy voice answered. At least it was summer, and the windows of the house were open, making a phone ringing in a shanty a couple hundred feet away easily heard.

"Whitney, would you mind taking me by a house about five miles from here and give me a few minutes to visit?" She pulled Levi's address out of her purse and handed it to her.

Whitney looked at the address. "Not at all."

Rumors had begun to swirl through the community about Levi's injury. Mammi had received three phone calls, and an Amish neighbor stopped by to tell her about it. The reports said "a woman" called an ambulance for him. That meant Levi had kept his word. He hadn't revealed who'd helped him, or at least it appeared that way.

Neither Mammi nor Sadie's parents had been home when she'd

returned last night, so they didn't know she'd gone out. This morning Sadie tended to the animals in the barn before Mammi Lee or Daed could. When her Daed wanted to go to the barn to hitch Bay to a rig, she volunteered to do that too. Anything to avoid answering questions about the strange thoroughbred in Mammi's barn. She didn't mind avoiding telling the truth. Adults had few people they told everything to. Even Jesus didn't tell everything to everyone. And she didn't have a problem trying to get her way when she felt God had given her the right to do so. But answering dishonestly wasn't something she could justify.

When Daed, Mamm, and Mammi had left today to visit Mammi's sister for the afternoon, Sadie had ridden Bay to Levi's and led Amigo home. But no one was there, so she put Amigo out to pasture and left.

As they continued toward Levi's, Sadie pondered all that had taken place last night. When the car braked, it pulled her from her thoughts.

"If you're going to be a few minutes, I have an errand I'd like to run."

"Sure. I'll be ready when you return."

Sadie went to the front door and knocked. Through the screen door she saw a young boy running toward her. He had silky blond hair and was wearing dark blue pants, a bright green shirt, red suspenders, and white socks with no shoes. For an Amish boy, he was wearing quite a mix of colors.

"Are you here to see Uncle Levi?" He skidded to a stop at the door. "Did he meet you at last night's singing? He didn't want to go, and I'm not sure he likes girls." The boy crossed his arms. "You look okay to me."

"Denki."

"Tobias." A thin man with curly brown hair and a beard walked up behind him. "That's not what you say to someone at the door, Son."

Tobias unfolded his arms. "What, that she looks okay or that Uncle Levi ain't fond of girls?"

"Both." The man opened the door. "*Kumm rei.* I'm Andy, and this is my son, Tobias."

"I'm Sadie, and I wanted—"

"You ain't from around here, are you?"

"Tobias." Andy put an index finger over his son's mouth before looking at Sadie with an apology. "He's very observant and feels the need to voice all his thoughts, however off-center they are."

"I like that." She grinned at Tobias. "I would like to see your uncle Levi."

Tobias frowned. "Are you the woman who helped him, the one who called last night and woke us up?"

"Of course not." Andy laughed. "Your uncle would have said if the person was Amish." Andy studied Sadie for a moment, and she tried to make her expression neutral. But when she saw realization dawn on his face, she knew she hadn't been fast enough. He grinned, a welcoming thankfulness radiating from him. "We owe you a great deal of thanks."

She shook her head, unsure whether she should admit she was the mystery woman. But dishonesty was not among her many faults. "I didn't know where I was when I stumbled upon him, and I certainly wouldn't have been riding through someone's hayfield had I realized what it was."

"Then I'm glad God used you. Old Man Hostetler told us a few weeks back he wouldn't be cutting that field again this year. I'm sure that's why Levi was there too."

He looked down and wiped sweat from his brow. "I got to the hospital before sunrise and spoke with a doctor not long after. Since that conversation I've been haunted by how things could have turned out." His brow furrowed. "When I returned home, I saw Amigo in the pasture."

"I tethered Amigo and rode my horse here earlier today, but no one was home." She glanced out the screen door. "My driver will return in a few minutes, and I would like to see Levi before I leave Apple Ridge."

"He's pretty groggy and not himself. He's a little more…bold and outspoken about what he's thinking and feeling."

"I can deal with that."

Tobias planted his feet and put his hands on his hips. "Uncle Levi's sleeping, and he said not to wake him up."

"You should listen to your uncle." Sadie touched the end of his nose, half expecting him to take a step back or complain. He didn't. "But I'm going to wake him." She looked at Andy. "Which way?"

Tobias looked at his Daed, and Andy nodded.

"Follow me." The little boy took off running and skidded to a stop several feet from a bed set up in the living room. "Don't touch the bed. Uncle Levi said to stay three feet away." Tobias held his hands apart, looking as if he were telling a fish story. "That's about this far. And he meant what he said."

"I'm sure he did." She couldn't believe how pale and stiff Levi looked. His left leg was in a full cast. A neck brace was fitted tight against his jawline. The base of the brace—a three-to-four-inch flat, circular piece—covered his chest and shoulders.

She turned to Andy. "I didn't expect this."

"It's an odd injury. He has a tiny neck fracture, and the doctor said it's the kind that can worsen until a person feels his arms and legs go numb. He could have done permanent damage. The kind that might have left him paralyzed from the neck down. As it is, Levi should be in a wheelchair in a week and on crutches later. He'll have to wear the neck brace for three to six months. The leg cast should be off in six weeks."

Sadie remembered Levi's pleas to help him up. God's mercy had surely extended to both of them last night.

Last night she'd seen that Levi was long and lanky with big shoulders. Now she could see his thick, curly hair, light brown with streaks of golden blond. It needed cutting—probably two months ago—but she liked his rugged, unkempt look. It meant that he, much like herself, wasn't interested in keeping every Amish rule of thumb.

His bed was midway between two double windows on opposite walls, inviting a cross breeze to cover him. But July afternoons weren't much for stirring air. A sheet lay over his uninjured leg and covered his hips and chest, but he looked uncomfortably warm, even without a shirt.

Levi shifted and groaned.

Sadie leaned over the bed, staring into his face. "Every time I see you, you're lying around and moaning."

His eyes remained closed, but a faint smile crossed his face. "Sadie." His gravelly voice was barely above a whisper and told of his exhaustion and, no doubt, of whatever pain medicine he was administered. "You *are* real."

"Ya, but I'm no angel."

The lines of pleasure deepened on his face. "And for that I'm very grateful."

If she'd been as angelic as her Daed wished, she wouldn't have been out last night or found Levi. Was he the reason she'd felt so moved during her prayers to saddle Bay and ride? Or had her own will been at work and stumbling across Levi was an odd coincidence?

"Tobias." Andy motioned to his son to leave the room with him. "Sadie, it was good meeting you."

"Denki." Where was the man's wife? In fact, now that she thought about it, it seemed odd Levi never mentioned his sister-in-law when they talked last night.

Andy started to leave, then turned back to her. "We're going to tend to the horses, but I'd rather Levi not be alone for too long. Just let me know when you're leaving by having your driver toot the horn."

"Be glad to."

"Andy." Levi's hoarse whisper brought his brother to a stop. Levi scrunched his face and opened his eyes for a moment. "A woman helped me last night, not Sadie." In the Amish community, one referred to people as Amish when they were such. The lack of that title would do exactly what Levi knew it would: indicate an Englisch woman had helped him.

Sadie appreciated Levi's sense of honor and his attempt to protect her.

Andy nodded, but questions filled his eyes.

Sadie shrugged. "I was grounded for the evening."

Andy's eyes narrowed, possibly thinking the same thing she did—she was too old for a parent to ground her. "It's not right for me to say it,"—Andy put his hands on Tobias's shoulders—"but I'm with Levi on this. I'm grateful you're no angel." He and Tobias left the room. A few moments later the screen door slammed.

His eyes still closed, Levi made a weak pat on the edge of his bed. She hesitated, but it seemed harmless with him injured and unable to speak much or keep his eyes open. They only had a few minutes to talk and were not likely to see each other again, so she sat.

He drew a heavy breath. "I was sure you'd already left Apple Ridge and I'd have no way to thank you."

She realized he was right. As determined as he was to keep her secret, he wouldn't have gone to her grandmother's to find out where she lived or how to reach her.

He tried to sit upright, and she helped by putting pillows behind him.

"Now." He eased back and waited for her to sit again. "Let's see those eyes."

She opened them wide.

"Hmm. You have big eyes."

"All the better to see you with." She waggled her eyebrows.

He laughed, then moaned. "No, not like a wolf. I meant they're large and pretty, somewhere between pale green and golden brown."

Sadie knew they weren't pretty, but she didn't believe he was trying to flatter her. He was just grateful to her, and gratitude changed people's views of everything they looked at. When she spent time in the Andes, soaking in the beauty of God's creation and fully aware of how poor and yet content the villagers were, her heart overflowed with gratitude. She learned then that the Daniels of the world—the ones she'd thought were better than her—were really no better or worse. The only thing that mattered was the honor and joy of walking with God.

Levi stretched his hand toward her face and ran his index finger across the bridge of her nose. "You have freckles."

Sadie found his observation a little amusing and intimidating. Her looks weren't a favorite subject. But she had no doubt his boldness to touch her was due to the medication he was taking.

He smiled, pinching her chin between his thumb and index finger. "You're very cute in a 'sunshine after the rain' sort of way."

She didn't know what he meant by that, but feelings fluttered through her, each tugging in a different direction. She'd grown out of being homely and horribly skinny. But she was no Aquilla. That was for sure. Still, she no longer felt she was less than other people.

"If you keep up this inspection, I'm going to demand you close your eyes and go to sleep."

"I can't help it." His dark brown eyes spoke of approval and friendship. "I've spent most of my waking minutes and half of my sleeping ones trying to imagine what you looked like and hoping you weren't an apparition."

She fidgeted, not sure she liked where this conversation was heading. Thankfully, she had to go soon. "It wouldn't be such a bad thing for me not to have been human. It'd mean you received help from God."

"I did receive help from God. He sent you to me."

Her muscles tensed, and she moved, ready to stand and say good-bye.

"Relax, Sadie." He put his hand on her arm. "You're gonna have to trust me when I say I'll be just as single when I die as I am today. We're alike in our determination to avoid marrying, so don't get your hackles up."

She took a deep breath. "Gut. You scared me for a minute."

He grimaced, looking hot and uncomfortable. Damp curls clung to his forehead.

Sadie fidgeted with the blanket. "Someone called Mammi's place today and said you had a concussion along with your other injuries."

"Ya, between that and the medicines, nothing feels real. But I want to get your address."

"Levi." She brushed his hair back, hoping it made him feel a little cooler. "We're saying all that needs to be said right now. I want to let it go at that."

"Knock, knock."

At the sound of a female voice behind them, Sadie pulled back her hand from Levi's face and stood.

Two young and attractive women stood at the open entryway of the living room, one holding a glass cake stand that encased a beautifully decorated cake.

Sadie turned to Levi, determined to speak softly so the others couldn't hear her. "Now that you're too injured to run away or ride off, you may be engaged in time for the wedding season."

Levi chuckled and slowly motioned for the women to enter, a movement that indicated how drugged he was. "These are my cousins Beth and Mattie. And this is Sadie. She returned my horse."

Sadie shook hands with the women. Levi's words were true enough. She *had* returned his horse. The odds were good that people who knew Levi had seen her on her trek to return Amigo. Levi had just given all the explanation anyone would need.

He scratched his jaw where the neck brace rubbed it. "Beth is a Hertzler of Hertzlers' Dry Goods."

Had they seen her sitting on Levi's bed and brushing the hair from his face? She hoped not. "When I was younger, I came to your store a couple of times with Mammi Lee."

"Verna Lee? The toymaker's wife?"

"Ya."

"We used to carry your *Grossdaadi*'s goods."

"I remember."

Beth touched Mattie's arm. "Mattie is working at the store now. She owned a cake shop in Ohio, so she's running her own bakery section here. Our husbands built a small café for her inside the store."

"A dry goods store with fresh cakes?"

"And sticky buns, scones, muffins, and lots of coffee." Mattie walked to a side table and set the cake on it. "It's about the size of a small bedroom, and I only have those other items as refreshments for the customers. The true heart of my business is using that space to showcase and take orders for decorative cakes. You know, for birthdays and weddings and such."

"Sounds as if Hertzlers' has changed a good bit since I was there more than ten years ago."

"Definitely," Beth said. "You should come by."

"Sadie knows a thing or two about stores, don't you?"

If Sadie could, she'd give him a glare for putting her on the spot. "A little, I guess. I help manage a five-and-dime run by a Mennonite couple. Aside from a few nonperishable items my two girlfriends and I make, the store carries the same things they did sixty years ago—including hayseed and shovels and such."

Beth moved to the foot of the bed. "What kinds of things do you make, Sadie?"

"When time and money allow, I make an assortment of things. I dabble in wreaths, but my favorites are candles and soaps, and when I can collect enough scraps of material from the Amish community where I live, I make cloth dolls."

Beth pulled a business card from her hidden apron pocket. "If you ever have a surplus and are looking for a place to sell them, come see me."

"Denki." Sadie took the card and touched the bed. "Levi, I need to go."

"Not without leaving your address and phone number."

Beth and Mattie looked at each other, a definite glimmer of interest passing between them.

Mattie fetched pen and paper from an end table and passed it to Sadie.

What could it hurt for him to have her address and phone number?

Nine

*L*evi stood in the round pen. He held a thirty-foot line in one hand and a lightweight longe whip in the other. Despite the neck brace he wore, he turned in circles with the horse on the other end of the line, training the animal to understand and follow his commands. *"Geh."*

The horse picked up its pace.

Even though Blaze hadn't been training long, the colt moved more fluidly and even paced than Levi could. Still, it was far easier for Levi to get around now that the cast on his leg had been removed a mere two days ago. He moved like an old man in winter while he sweated under the grueling August sun.

Levi needed to make up for lost training time. *"Langsam."* Blaze didn't slow a tad. "Langsam," Levi repeated in the same even tone. The horse raised its head and altered its pace a little. "Gut... Langsam."

"Uncle Levi." Tobias sat on the split-rail fence and pointed at the whip. "You gotta at least let him see that out of the corner of his eye."

"Who's doing the training? Me or you?"

Tobias clutched a hand to the top of his head. "But you're *not* listening to me."

"You're being impatient again." When Levi had been on crutches, he'd had to enlist Tobias's help to tend and train the horses. The boy had a knack for handling the stout and sometimes difficult creatures, but he lacked patience with the tedious process.

"So who got throwed by a horse? Me or you?"

"I have a better question, peanut. Who's going to be sent inside if he doesn't stop telling me what to do?" Levi knew that threat would carry some weight. Tobias liked being in his or Andy's shadow at all times. Since Andy was in the barn tending to the other horses, if Tobias had to go inside, he'd be by himself.

Tobias made monkey gestures in the air, touching the top of his head and flailing his arms, huffing and making mocking gestures—but in all his silliness, he didn't say anything. For almost a minute. "Not everybody thinks you need to go as slow as you do with training horses, Uncle Levi."

"What's their motivation for feeling that way? Because it's what's best for the horse and the buyer or because it's what's easiest and most profitable for the trainer?"

Tobias frowned but seemed to mull over the question.

Amigo had been five years old when Daniel bought him last spring from an auction. Levi didn't know why the horse reacted so violently to the fireworks last month, but he'd learned some valuable lessons, ones that caused him and Andy to start training their horses differently. One brother fed the animal and soothed him while the other made an awful racket just outside the barn—beating a horseshoe against a ten-gallon tub, yelling and clapping, or sounding an old car horn. The technique seemed to be desensitizing the animals to loud noises, but it was too early to tell if that would translate to a calmer horse on a road.

"Look." Tobias pointed at the mailman pulling onto the gravel driveway. He hopped down. "Whatcha want to guess he's got another package from your girlfriend?"

Levi continued working with Blaze, but he hoped the man did have another package from Sadie. She needed money for her mission trip, and he wanted to do all he could to help her. He'd put some of the life-sized cloth dolls she sewed in his handcrafted cradles and highchairs. When the two items were combined, they sold like hotcakes at Hertzlers'.

He also enjoyed the short letters that accompanied her packages. When he first came up with the idea of her making dolls to go with some of his toy furniture, he called her. But she wasn't keen on the idea of partnering with him. It'd taken a few phone calls before he could sufficiently assure her that he was only interested in being a friend and repaying his debt to her.

Dealing with her was like working with a spooked horse. At first he thought she'd been in a relationship that had gone bad. But after coming to know her a little better, he understood that her heart belonged to the people in a remote Peruvian village, and she was determined to stay the course.

Tobias took the package from the man and held it up. "Ya, it's from her."

"Gut." He'd never known anyone like Sadie.

Just as the mailman pulled out of the driveway, he saw another vehicle coming in. Daniel rolled down the passenger window and waved.

Levi returned the wave. "Tobias, go put that on my bed before anything happens to it." The dolls' faces, arms, and legs were made of white cotton, and if they were smudged, they didn't sell as easily.

Tobias tore out running.

Levi didn't expect Daniel this week. Then again, Daniel may not have known himself until the mood struck him to head this way.

The truck came to a halt, and Daniel got out. "A man without a cast on his leg." Daniel shook Levi's hand and patted his shoulder at the same time. "Still got that noose around your neck, I see. How you feeling?"

"Lighter now." Levi ran two fingers around the top collar of the brace. "And ready to be free of this yoke around my neck."

"Sure you are. You're gettin' there. It's been a hot summer to have to wear that thing while working."

The screen door flung open, and Tobias ran outside.

Daniel didn't seem to notice the boy. He motioned to his driver, Tip. "I heard there are some good horses going on the block tonight at Toppers. I'd sure like it if you could join me."

"Your eye for buying horses at auction is much better than mine."

"Ya, but you're better at knowing which one should go to which trainer."

Andy emerged from the barn. "Daniel, I didn't know you were here...or even coming."

"I'm not staying. We'll talk horse-trading another time. But I'm hoping to borrow Levi for a bit."

Daniel called it horse-trading, but what he meant was buying the animals at auction, bringing them to Levi to train, selling them to people throughout the region, and settling up with the Fisher brothers what was owed. Nobody worried about a timetable for the payments. Daniel's word was good enough, and he was more than fair when it came to paying people for their services, but he did things in his own way and time.

Tobias bounced up and down. "Can I go?"

"Not this time, champ." Daniel pushed down on the top of Tobias's straw hat. "We might not be home until the wee hours of the morning, and if we arrive that late, your uncle will need some sleep, and your Daed will need your help tending to the horses the next morning." Daniel pulled a five-dollar bill from his billfold. "You'll agree to work for me, ya?"

"Wow." Tobias took the money, staring at it with wide eyes. "I'm available anytime."

"Gut. I'm glad to hear it."

It dawned on Levi that by going to Toppers, he'd be fifteen to twenty minutes from Sadie's place in Stone Creek. "What time does the horse auction begin?"

"Around eight, most likely. Of course, as usual, you and Tip will stay at Toppers while I find some lonely girl to take to dinner."

Daniel's dating habits were questionable at best, but at least he seemed to be trying to find someone. Still, it seemed odd how quickly Daniel could connect with a woman only to lose interest within the same evening.

Daniel's plans aside, it was around one now, and it'd take two hours to get there. If Sadie were home, that meant he could visit with her for a couple of hours before the horses were on the block. Daniel didn't need him to help buy the horses, only to pair each animal with a trainer.

"Levi?"

He looked at Daniel. "Sure. Just let me jump in the shower. I'll be ready in ten minutes." He headed for the house.

"The horses don't care what you smell like," Daniel hollered.

"Ten minutes." Levi hurried into the house, hoping he would see Sadie tonight.

Ten

The wooden floors of the old store creaked as Sadie carried a large sign to the window. She taped it to the glass: For Sale.

It seemed as if her hopes of having enough money to go back to Peru hung in the balance more than ever, teetering under the weight of yet another unexpected change in her world.

She turned, taking a long look around her, enjoying the sights and smells of the old-fashioned place. In her mind's eye she could see Loyd and Edna the day she'd wandered in here. She'd said she was looking for work, but she needed so much more than that. She'd been broken and mortified by Daniel. Although she hadn't told Loyd or Edna about her former fiancé, they seemed to understand what she needed and took her under their wing. At the same time, they taught her how to earn a living while her heart mended.

Now, as unexpectedly as a summer storm, Loyd had fallen ill, and Edna insisted on getting out from under the pressure of running the store.

"Sadie." Blanche, her coworker and a roommate, held up a large cardboard box. "Do you need another one?"

Edna had told them to get all their crafts off the shelves and to return what they could to the manufacturers. After some advertising, they would put everything else into a one-day-only, going-out-of-business sale.

"Ya. Denki." She took the box and moved to the candle aisle.

Edna insisted on rearranging her life so she didn't have to focus on anything but Loyd. The elderly woman had been ready to be free of the store for a long time, but Loyd enjoyed the work too much to let it go. Edna hadn't set foot inside Farmers' Five-and-Dime since Loyd's stroke two weeks ago, because she hadn't left his side for a moment.

Sadie pulled jars of her homemade candles off the shelves. Seeing Edna and Loyd like this made her ache all over, confirming her suspicion: life was easier if one never let in anyone else. If two hearts grow to become one, what happens when one stops beating? Sure, Loyd and Edna had good fruit to show for their years together, but today's heartache seemed to weigh heavier than all the harvests of yesteryear.

Maybe she was wrong. She hoped so, for the sake of all who'd ever married.

Someone tapped at the front door.

"I'll get it." Blanche headed that way.

They had a huge sign on the door that said Closed, but people knocked on the door anyway. This old place had been open six days a week since the early fifties.

Old habits died hard.

"Sadie," Blanche called, "there's a man here to see you. I didn't recognize him, so I told him to wait outside."

Sadie went toward the glass door. Her eyes widened as she reached for the handle. The man was facing the other way, with his hat in his hand, but there was no mistaking those loose curls of golden-brown hair. Of course, if his hair wasn't a dead giveaway, there was the neck brace too. A smile tugged at her mouth for the first time in quite a while. She opened the heavy door, and the bells suspended over the entryway clanged as she stepped outside.

He turned awkwardly, having to move his whole body because of the neck brace. There was a smile on his tan face, but what she noticed most of all was the spark in his eyes.

Sadie put her hands on her hips. "Well, look at you, standing on your own two feet."

"Hard to believe, isn't it?"

"It is indeed." She'd heard energy in his voice when they spoke on the phone, but this was the first time she could see vitality in his expression.

They moved away from the door, going a little farther onto the sidewalk as if they wanted some privacy. "What are you doing here?"

"There's a horse auction nearby."

"Decided to sell Amigo and get a new friend, did you?"

He chuckled. "No, nothing like that. Just helping a friend make some decisions. He doesn't need me for a while, so I had the driver drop me off at your place. I walked here from there."

"Good thing I was findable, or you'd be calling that driver to come back. You do have your phone, right?"

"Still there." He tapped his pocket. "I took a chance, figuring if you could find me in a dark field without trying, I could find you in a small town if I were willing to do a little searching."

"Gotta appreciate a man with confidence."

"I was right, wasn't I?"

"It's my understanding that you did indeed find me…I think."

Faint dimples appeared when he grinned. Heat radiated from the white concrete, and she considered asking him to step inside.

His expression became thoughtful, and his smile faded. He pointed at the For Sale sign in the window. "What's going on?"

"Loyd, the owner, had a stroke a couple of weeks back."

"I'm sorry to hear that. Why didn't you say something about that?" He sounded concerned, perhaps for how this would affect her.

"Truth is, until a few days ago, I couldn't make myself talk about it, not on the phone or in a letter. I finally wrote you about it. You'll get a package soon with a letter explaining what's going on."

"Oh, ya. I received one today, but I didn't get a chance to open it."

"Now you don't have to. Although you may wish you'd read it rather than hear me whine about how this stinks for Loyd and Edna, the town folk, my roommates, and…"

"You."

"Sorry, I can be really selfish at times."

"I know you're hurting for the Farmers, but this has to put pressure on you too. I can't see where it's selfish to admit to feeling the strain." He shifted. "I saw that there's a rodeo demonstration and fair at the park. I think a lot of people are starting to leave now. Would you care to see what we can?"

"It's Stone Creek Day at Stone Creek Lake. They have booths of crafts and a petting zoo with farm animals, some blow-up bounce castles for the children, and other family stuff."

"Stone Creek Lake?" He tugged lightly at the neck brace. "What's next, Stone Creek River?"

"Ya. We have that too."

"Of course you do." His grin made the tan lines around his eyes disappear.

"Stone Creek River starts about five miles south of here. If you named horses like they named places around here, you could have an Amigo Friend." She raised an eyebrow, trying to keep a silly smile off her face.

"Or an Enemy Enemigo."

"A river by any name would flow just as deep and swift and surely sparkle just as much under the August sun." Her goal to keep a straight face while teasing him was impossible.

"Did you just twist Shakespeare?"

"Are you an Amish man who knows Shakespeare?"

"I know all there is to know, which boils down to maybe three lines. That was one of them."

She giggled. "That's all there is to know?"

"That's more than I'll need in this lifetime."

"True, and your knowledge about equals mine." She broke into a grin. How fun to be able to talk with him whether he was injured in a field, in the living room of his home, on the phone, or here. "But Shakespeare must've been quite a writer for people like us to quote his work some four hundred years later."

"Never thought about it. But I can tell you something I have thought about"—he wiped sweat from his forehead—"getting under some shade trees."

It was hard to believe, but she liked the idea of spending a little time with Levi. "I'll be right back." She went inside the store and told her roommates she'd meet them at the house later. Edna had given each of them an area of the store to pack up, and as long as she got hers done before Monday, it didn't matter when she did it. She hurried out the door, grateful for the distraction.

Levi pulled his attention from the random items displayed in the store's window. "Ready?"

"Ya."

They walked down the sidewalks of the historic downtown. After a while they stepped into a café and ordered a couple of cold drinks to go. The conversation stayed light as they discussed the weather, Tobias, how well their handiwork was selling, and how Levi was progressing with the training of a yearling. It seemed as if Levi knew she couldn't talk about what really weighed on her. Not yet.

She had tough decisions to make now that the store was closing, and talking about them with someone who had nothing to gain, no reason to try to steer her one way or the other, was like a godsend.

But was he as he appeared, or was she so desperate for answers she was seeing what she wanted to? She prayed, asking for guidance on whether to turn to Levi for advice.

They meandered across the thick grass of the park, watching as some people were dismantling their booths. Children milled about with leashed dogs. Across the way, men led horses to trailers while other workmen dismantled the arena that had been set up so riders could demonstrate some of the stunts they would perform at next month's rodeo.

Levi took a sip of his orange soda. "Looks as if maybe you shoulda set up a booth here to sell your goods."

"The city doesn't allow the town shops to set up booths for Stone Creek Day. Since I work for Farmers' and they sell my stuff there, I fall under the can't-have-a-booth category." She played with the straw in her cup, poking at some ice chips. "I was boxing up the last of my craft items when you showed up."

"I could take them back with me. Beth would be happy to put them on consignment in her store."

Sadie paused, staring at him. That was a great offer—if she could snatch it up and not analyze it to death.

Levi lowered his drink. "You have a look on your face like the one I get when I'm baffled by a horse's behavior and unsure what to do to get him to do what I want him to do."

If he was this intuitive with his horses, he was no doubt a remarkable trainer. "I'm sort of baffled by all of life right now."

"Been there a dozen times. Want to tell me about it?"

She did, but the idea of actually sharing her thoughts made her squirm. What if his opinion affected her final decision and he was wrong? "Maybe later."

They remained there, a few yards from the lake, taking in the sights. A cooling breeze played with the strings to her prayer Kapp. A baby cooed nearby, and she searched for it.

A few feet away a woman sat on a blanket with a little one dressed in pink and wearing a silky headband. The baby girl was about six months old. She sat on her mother's lap. The woman smiled at her child. "Is that right?" She waited for the baby to respond. "You tell Mommy all about it."

The baby seemed mesmerized by her mother, cooing as if her tender sounds actually formed words. A toddler in a beige dress was asleep on the blanket next to the woman and her baby. The mom brushed black hair off the sleeping child's neck, her face glowing, as if this moment made up for all the nights of walking the floors while her little ones wailed.

Sadie and Levi headed toward the lake. Behind them a huge ruckus broke out. Men and women shrieked, yelling words Sadie couldn't make out. Some were grabbing their children and scattering. A man's voice rose above the clamor. "Stop him! Somebody grab a rein!"

A black horse appeared out of nowhere and thundered toward them. Sadie slung her drink to the ground.

Levi grabbed her hand, and in one fell swoop, he tugged her forward and forced her arms straight out, as if she were a scarecrow. "Stay." Despite his neck brace and not being able to turn his head, he took off running, pointing to people as he went. "Get behind a tree!"

People scattered, obeying his command. The path cleared—all except for Sadie, who stood like a target.

Everything was happening fast. Maybe six or eight seconds had passed since the chaos began. Sadie's head whirled the way it had when she was a child and her Daed spun her by her arms around and around, her little legs gliding through the air.

Levi disappeared behind a tree—and she was standing in the horse's path! Was he *crazy*?

The massive creature charged straight at her. Earth flew from its rumbling hoofs, but she couldn't budge.

A moment later Levi lunged forward, grabbing the horse's rein before throwing himself onto its neck. In a flash he was atop the animal. "Whoa!" Levi's voice carried calm firmness while she wanted to scream like a banshee—if only she could find her voice.

"Whoa!" He pulled on the reins, and the horse slowed, prancing as it did, finally coming to a halt twenty feet from her.

When Sadie could take her eyes off the horse, she looked behind her. Levi had put her ten feet in front of the blanket with the mother and two children. If the horse had gotten past him, he'd intended for her to scare it away from that spot. The mom had gotten to her feet, terror on her face, with the baby clutched in her arms. If the horse had kept coming, Sadie doubted the mother and child could have gotten to safety. What if she'd tried to grab her toddler first?

Impossible.

Sadie's heart pounded. "Are you okay?"

The woman sank to her knees, rocking her little one. "Yeah." The toddler awoke, unaware of what had happened. She brushed sweat-matted hair from her face and crawled into her mother's arms, next to the baby.

"Thank you!" another voice said. It was the same one that had begged for someone to stop the horse.

Sadie searched for the speaker.

A large man was struggling to breathe as he made his way toward them. He waved toward Levi, not that Levi saw him. "I'll be there as soon as…" His voice faded while he gasped for air.

Levi eased off the horse, moving much slower than when he'd gotten on. Had he hurt himself? He held the reins, stroking the horse and talking to it in a low, soothing voice. When Levi came toward Sadie, he led the horse. Levi put his free hand on his chest before moving it to her shoulder. "That was scary. Much more so than me landing in a hayfield."

He'd thought so clearly, covering possibilities that were just now dawning on her. If he'd simply scared the horse away from the woman on the blanket with her two little ones, the rampaging animal could have trampled other children or even adults. By hiding behind the tree, he avoided scaring the horse and sending him off in a different direction.

Sadie's legs shook, and she looked for a place to sit. She needed a few moments to absorb what had just happened. Her first thought when he moved into action was outrage that he'd dared to put her in harm's way while protecting himself. She couldn't have been more wrong.

"I think I hate horses."

"Don't do that." He patted the horse's neck. "They're like people—good hearts, occasional bad judgment, and sometimes volatile reactions when scared." Levi tilted his head, studying her eyes before he smiled. "You'll be fine in a bit. I can see it."

She drew a deep breath, surprised to find that she believed him despite how she felt.

"Excuse me."

They turned at the man's voice to find the woman from the blanket standing next to a man who now held the sleepy toddler. "I can't thank you enough." The man's voice cracked. "You did that for us, and you've got a neck injury." The man shook Levi's hand.

For the next few minutes, people gushed over Levi, thanking him and asking if he was okay. The owner retrieved his horse, also grateful for what Levi had done. When the man learned what Levi did for a living, he asked for a business card, and Levi gave him one.

Sadie and Levi moved to a bench that faced the lake, neither one talking. He had to be more drained than she was. The dad of the two little ones brought them cold drinks and a bag of popcorn.

Sadie opened the can of Sprite. "Did you hurt your neck?"

Levi set his drink on the bench between them. "I don't think so." He opened the popcorn and held it for her. "This collar is like wearing a cast. It protects against another break while allowing the healing to continue."

"That's good."

They grew still, staring at the lake for a long time. Her thoughts drifted. Surely a man who reacted in the best interests of innocent bystanders could be trusted with her puny problems.

Ducks waddled over to them, and she tossed bits of popcorn and watched sunlight sparkle on the water.

She ate a few pieces of popcorn. "When Daed finds out about the store closing, he'll insist I come home." She tossed a few more pieces onto the ground.

"Would moving in with Mammi Lee be any easier for you?"

"It's possible. She doesn't seem as bent out of shape about my not being married, but Daed won't tolerate it. It'd be an insult for me to be unemployed and homeless and still not return home. I can't afford for him to feel like I'm totally rebelling against him."

"I can understand how he'd feel that way."

"Me too, but I don't want to move back home." She sighed. "I have no job. Loyd and Edna paid a portion of our rent each month, but now Blanche is moving back home. That'll make our rent even higher. If I stay, I might be able to get another job, but I'll plow through everything that I've saved so far for my mission trip."

"I can't offer much advice, but I can tell you how I'd think this through."

"Please."

"I'd keep my focus on the goal. Yours is Peru. Avoiding living with your parents is a perk, not your ambition. Stay true to what's most important. Seems to me that since you're no longer working at the five-and-dime, you can reduce your bills by living at home and using your time to make crafts."

"You think if I made that many more crafts, I could actually sell them?"

"Seems likely. You just need to get them into every store possible. Beth can help you with that. She keeps several stores, both Amish and Englisch, supplied with Amish goods."

Sadie took another sip of her drink. The idea of moving home wasn't her favorite, but she had to admit, looking at the big picture as Levi suggested, it made sense. Of course, while she was there, her parents and the community would do all they could to spark a relationship between her and one of the single Amish men.

Too bad Levi didn't have an answer for that.

Eleven

Using tiny wooden pegs, Levi attached another brace to the bottom of a cradle. He needed to take a load of goods to Hertzlers' soon. He had a meeting set up for one o'clock. Later this afternoon, around three, Daniel was supposed to drop off some horses for training and pick up others that were ready to be sold. The process would take the rest of the day, perhaps until midnight.

The door to the shop creaked, and he raised his head. The neck brace made his workday harder because it was hot and unforgiving, but he tried not to let it grate on his nerves. He was healing, and that was all that really mattered.

Andy had a box in his hand. "This came for you."

"Denki. Just set it on the counter." He tapped the last peg into place and turned the cradle upright. "The stuff lined up against the wall is ready to go. Could you hitch up the wagon and pull it around?" Grabbing a sheet of fine sandpaper, he noticed that Andy lingered by the door. "Is there a problem?" Levi scrubbed the headboard, causing wood particles to swirl in the air.

He hoped nothing was wrong. He had neither the time nor the patience for any issues today.

"Mamm came by earlier to see if you'd heard from Sadie."

"And now I have." Levi removed a cotton rag from his pants pocket and used it to wipe off the headboard. He inspected the finished product, smoothing a few rough spots with sandpaper.

Despite Levi's request that Andy pitch in, he continued to wait by the door. Andy opened his mouth twice and drew a quick breath as if on the verge of saying something. Levi turned the cradle upside down again, ready to attach the two rockers.

"If you've got something on your mind, say it. We have fifteen hours of work to do during the next five hours."

Andy picked up one of the finished toy highchairs and propped it on his shoulder. "You know Mamm and Daed think you and Sadie have something going on."

Levi threw the rag onto the table, studying his brother. "And?"

Andy tucked another chair under his arm and picked up a cradle. "Do you?"

Levi turned his back on Andy and grabbed a hand drill. "I don't know who's worse, you or them." After putting a seat for a toy highchair on the bench, he pulled out a measuring tape. "All I want is a little peace on this topic. Could you get the horse hitched up and everything loaded, please?"

The screen door slammed, leaving the silence to heap guilt on Levi.

Three weeks ago, after his visit with Sadie in Stone Creek, he'd ended up staying in a hotel with Daniel and the driver. The auction and subsequent sorting and hauling of horses had lasted until nearly dawn. When he'd arrived at Andy's around noon the next day and stepped out of the car with a couple of boxes of Sadie's crafts, his folks were there.

Their parents lived across the back pasture, so it wasn't unusual for them to pop in, often with food for the bachelors. They were good people, and Levi loved them and enjoyed their company—when they weren't matchmaking. But since he had Sadie's boxes in tow, they had questions. He couldn't figure out how to avoid admitting he'd gone by to see the woman who'd returned his horse. So he told them the truth—he'd gone to see her, discovered the five-and-dime was closing, and planned to give her crafts to Beth for the store.

Neither Mamm nor Daed had asked any more questions. They simply nodded, but Levi recognized the look in his mother's eyes, and he couldn't douse it. She was a good woman whose heart had broken when Andy's wife had left. She believed if Levi didn't marry, he'd be worse off than Andy, because he'd die without ever having loved someone or having children or grandchildren.

Her ache for Andy and Levi was like a hole in her gentle heart.

Then Sadie sent another package of dolls, but also inside the box was a gift for him. It was a simple gesture, a candle shaped like a horse and made to smell of leather, but Tobias saw it and ran across the field to tell his grandparents that Levi's girlfriend was sending him presents.

The sound of horse hoofs and the creaking wagon let Levi know his brother was back. The screen door opened again. "Hey, Levi."

"Ya?"

Andy didn't say anything, and Levi turned to face him.

"You're annoyed with me, and I get that, but I carry this awful fear that my life has redirected yours in a negative way."

"Oh, all right. I'll load the stuff myself." Levi grabbed numerous pieces from along the wall. With a couple of cradles and a rocking horse in hand, he went out the door and to the nearby wagon.

"We're having a conversation here!" Andy followed him, carrying several more items.

The way Levi saw it, Andy's and Daniel's experiences had opened his eyes. That was a positive thing, not something Andy needed to feel bad about. But Levi knew his brother wouldn't see it that way. "You need to stop. Stop fretting. Just...stop!"

"Okay," Andy growled, setting the stuff in the wagon. "All I want to know is if you're courting Sadie. Just tell me straight up."

Levi stared at his brother, tempted to climb onto the wagon seat and drive off. "Look, I know what Mamm and Daed think, and maybe there's some whispering about Sadie and me in the community. But do you have any idea how nice it's been these last few weeks with no one prodding me about attending singings or making wisecracks about how I *can't* find a girl who'll have me? I'm sick of being needled about it." He removed his tool belt and threw it onto the porch of the workshop. "And you've joined them."

"Okay." Andy sighed and leaned his forearms against the wagon. "But it's been four years since you moved in with us to help me juggle work and raise Tobias, to help us cope with the hole Eva left, to make the house feel less lonely. You'll never know how much I appreciate that, but—"

"So?" Levi interrupted. "You want me to move out? Is that it?"

"Don't be ridiculous! For my sake, for Tobias's, being completely self-ish, I'd side with you about avoiding singings and staying single. I'd have you live here forever." Andy shook his head. "But I want what's best for you. Not what's best for me or even Tobias."

Levi climbed into the wagon and took the reins. "Then be my brother, my friend, and my business partner. But stop trying to be my trainer."

Twelve

Beth picked up a large stack of empty handwoven shopping baskets from the counter near the register. She went through the main part of the store, heading for the front to return them to their rightful spot. Zigzagging between small groups of shoppers, she enjoyed the breeze that flowed through the aisles, caressing her skin. It was the second week in September, and today was the first hint that summer was fading and autumn was on its way.

Jonah was descending a ladder, holding a large clock he'd removed from the wall display. He stepped off the last rung and passed the clock to an employee, giving instructions. He then grabbed his cane off the ladder's hinge. As Beth skirted around the customers, someone put a hand on her arm, and for a moment she thought a patron had a question. But then she recognized Jonah's tender touch. His golden-brown eyes stared into her soul, melting her right there in front of everyone—if the others hadn't been too busy to notice.

"I'll take those." He lifted the baskets from her arms and repositioned his cane, all without moving his gaze from hers. His lopsided grin tempted her to kiss him.

Jonah moved in closer. "How about if you and I take a break?" He brushed his lips near her ear. "I'll make us lunch and bring it to your office."

"I'd planned to grab a few bites of a sandwich while working. I'm backlogged on the inventory. I haven't logged or shelved the items that came in this morning, and Levi will be here soon with his goods."

"Please. Take just a few minutes to get off your feet and rest."

She slid her hand over her slightly protruding stomach. The bump was hardly noticeable to onlookers. Five months pregnant and each day she'd witnessed the joy of their news in her husband's eyes, a pleasure that seemed to know no bounds.

"I'm going to be spoiled before this child is born."

"I don't think sitting at lunchtime qualifies as being pampered."

"How about if we sit at one of the outdoor tables of Mattie Cakes café?"

"Is the shade of the white oak calling you again?"

She grinned. He knew her well. "It is."

"Beth," Lillian said.

"It's not the only voice calling to you." Jonah brushed his hand against hers, smiling as they turned to the girl behind the register.

Lillian held up jars of Amish candles. "When will we get some more of these?"

Jonah squeezed Beth's shoulder. "Lunch will be served in twenty minutes."

"I'll meet you there."

She went toward the customer who was buying the last of Sadie's candles. "I don't know." Beth had left several messages for Sadie on her parents' answering machine, but that was in a phone shanty. And as of yet Sadie hadn't returned any of her calls. She made a mental note to ask Levi about it when he came in later. Surely Sadie returned his calls. "But I'll do what I can to get some more."

Beth took notes on what the woman wanted, chatted with her for a bit, and then headed toward the café.

The chimes of several clocks bonged, letting her know it was half past noon, and then one of them played music. Beth continued through the craft supplies aisle, but she always savored the only source of music allowed in an Amish store or household. She and Jonah had one of these timepieces in their bedroom.

As Beth went through the little section of the store that was Mattie Cakes café, Mattie glanced up. "Need anything?"

Beth pointed toward the door several feet behind Mattie. "I'm having lunch on your patio as soon as Jonah arrives with it."

Mattie smiled. "It's a beautiful day, even if we haven't had a change of seasons yet." Mattie turned to a customer and opened her portfolio of celebration cakes. She pointed one out to the woman. "This is probably similar to what you described."

"Yes. It's perfect. You can make this?"

Beth smiled as she stepped outside. She paused near the doorway, letting her eyes adjust to the sunlight.

The patio was as new as the area they called Mattie Cakes café. There were three wrought-iron tables with a couple of chairs each and a short picket fence that connected to the store. Since the patio abutted the gravel parking lot, Jonah and Mattie's husband, Gideon, had put in the fence mostly to keep little ones from escaping and wandering into a driver's path.

It was so nice to have Mattie back. She had lived three years in Berlin, Ohio, with her brother. Unfortunately, the transition from Ohio back to Apple Ridge hadn't been easy for Mattie. She returned only because her cake shop there had burned down just before Thanksgiving last year, and her parents had insisted she come home for a while. Mattie had moved away because of a rift between Gideon and her, but once she was back home, she slowly learned of the great sacrifices he'd made to protect her from the trials he was going through. Once the truth was laid out, Mattie made it known that nothing short of death could ever keep her from Gideon again. They had married in March, and Beth had the pleasure of witnessing their love and joy make up for the time they'd been apart.

Jonah crossed the parking lot toward her, his cane in one hand and a tray in the other. It was convenient having a home only a stone's throw from the store.

She opened the gate and let him in. He'd made two sandwiches and put several types of fruit in a bowl.

"I'll get some water from Mattie." Jonah set the items on a table and pulled out a chair for her to prop up her feet. They were pretty good at snatching downtime together during the workday.

Before he could turn to enter the store, Mattie brought out two glasses. "Water, anyone?"

"Perfect." Jonah took them from her.

She went back inside as he sat down across from Beth. "So what's on your mind for Sunday afternoon?"

She shared her thoughts about having a picnic by the creek, and the conversation rolled along as if they hadn't seen each other in months. They both looked up when Levi pulled into the lot.

Beth stood. "This was nice."

Jonah got up and threw away the trash. "But work calls us back."

Levi toted an armload toward the service door. All three headed for the stockroom to check in the items.

"Hey, Levi. How are you today?" Jonah asked.

"Gut, and you?" Levi knew the routine well, so he lined up several pieces for check-in. He set a red barn trimmed in white on the floor.

"You've outdone yourself." Beth inspected the two-story building.

He'd created wooden fences and farm animals to boot. The tiny sheep were covered in real sheepskin, and the cows had strips of rawhide glued to their wooden bodies.

"Glad you like it." Levi nodded, and Beth could tell he was in no mood to talk. "I have some more pieces in the wagon."

"Let's bring them in." Jonah clasped his hand on Levi's shoulder.

Beth grabbed the inventory clipboard and a pen and began logging the new items.

Levi walked in carrying another cradle. "This isn't the full order we discussed last May. I'm working on another two-story dollhouse, but it and plenty of other stuff aren't done yet."

Beth couldn't stop her smile. "I may want to keep the dollhouse you're working on for our little one instead of selling it."

Jonah chuckled. "Our *son* won't appreciate a dollhouse."

No matter how she referred to their child, as a boy or a girl, he'd pick the opposite gender to make a remark. But he never favored one or the other, because it didn't matter to either of them. They wanted the child she was carrying. Period.

"Levi,"—Beth scribbled a few notes in the margin of the papers— "I've been trying to reach Sadie and haven't heard back from her. Next time you talk to her, would you ask her to call me?"

"I…don't know when that'll be." Levi separated the rungs of a rocking horse from the base of a highchair.

Beth's eyes met Jonah's. That's all Levi had to say? He was as guarded as they came. Consistently nice. Always polite. Quite humorous at times. But discovering what he really thought? Impossible.

A salesclerk called for Jonah, and he headed back into the store.

Beth returned her attention to the invoice. "Is this everything?"

Levi counted the objects. "I think there must be two more items in the wagon...or still at the house."

While he ran another quick count, Beth stepped to the doorway, thinking she might spot any items in the back of his rig. Bright sunshine greeted her, and she blinked to adjust her eyes. An Amish woman in a horse-drawn wagon was pulling into the store parking lot. That was fairly common. The Amish brought their wares to Hertzlers' regularly. But... She squinted, trying to see clearly.

"Levi." She turned back toward the stockroom. "I think you might be talking to Sadie today."

Levi joined Beth at the doorway. A broad smile changed his countenance, but she was pretty sure something else reflected in his eyes—almost as if he felt hesitant.

Thirteen

*A*s Sadie brought the wagon to a stop at the hitching post, she saw Levi coming toward her, and she couldn't help but smile.

He grinned. "What are you doing here?"

"I could ask you the same thing."

He tethered Bay to the post and patted her neck. "I was making a delivery."

She motioned to the boxes in the back of her wagon before climbing down.

Levi moved to the back of the wagon and unhitched the tailgate. "How long will you be in Apple Ridge?"

"Only for the weekend." She helped remove the tailgate and slid it into the wagon. "I've been home in Brim for only three weeks, and my parents are already on my last nerve. Since Beth left messages saying she needed these items right away, and it was about as cheap to hire a driver as it was to ship them here, I couldn't pass up the chance to get away for a bit and for as long as possible."

"Looks like you've been busy." He pulled several boxes toward him and began stacking them.

"I just hope I can make enough money to be on my way come December, because my parents are parading me around like a horse at auction." She reached farther back into the wagon and pulled a heavy box toward her.

Two Amish girls emerged from the same door Levi had come through a few minutes earlier.

Levi picked up a stack of boxes. "Are these marked with what's in them?"

"Ya. I wrote a code on the box tops." She pointed to the markings. "See, 'CLG16' means candles, large, in glass containers. There are sixteen in each box." She pulled another box toward her. "'SS36' means small soaps, thirty-six bars."

He gestured toward the women heading their way. "I'm sure Beth sent them to help unload. Why don't you stay at the wagon and tell them what's in each box. I'll clear out a spot in the stockroom so they can be grouped by kind. It'll make checking them in easier."

"Sure. Denki."

Levi smiled and gave a nod before disappearing with his stack of boxes.

Sadie climbed into the wagon and pushed more boxes toward the tailgate.

"Hi." A young woman waved. "Beth said you probably have some things we need to put on the shelves right away."

"Candles, soaps, wreaths, and dolls." Sadie got down and stacked several lightweight boxes. "These are wreaths."

The woman picked up the stack. "I'm Lillian. This is Katie."

"Nice to meet you. I'm Sadie."

Lillian's eyes grew wide, and she set the boxes back in the wagon. "Levi's Sadie?" She held out her hand. "It's nice to finally meet you."

"Denki." Sadie shook her hand, inwardly shooing away the thought of being called Levi's Sadie. There were so many Amish who shared the same name that they often referred to one another by nicknames. "I'm thrilled to have a place to sell my crafts."

"We are so glad you found Levi's horse." She giggled. "And found each other in the process."

Ready for Lillian to stop making her feel awkward about her friendship with Levi, Sadie edged in front of her and picked up the stack of boxes. She put them in Katie's hands. "These are wreaths," she repeated.

Katie grinned. "I'm with Lillian. It's great to meet you. All of Apple Ridge has been abuzz, and so few of us have ever met you." Katie turned and hurried into the store.

Concern and doubts over exactly what Levi was saying about her nagged at Sadie. She created a new stack of boxes and passed them to Lillian. "These are dolls, smaller than the ones Levi uses for the highchairs and cradles."

"Excellent." Lillian started to walk off.

"Lillian?"

The young woman turned.

"What's being said about me?"

"Not much. Just that you and Levi have been seeing each other since July." She shrugged a shoulder. "Levi's quite a catch, and everybody thinks it's wonderful he finally has a girlfriend."

Girlfriend? Sadie's heart knotted. Levi returned with Katie right behind him.

Lillian glanced at him and back to Sadie. "You don't mind that being said, do you?"

Levi clapped his hands once. "What do you have, Lillian?"

"Dolls, small ones."

"Put them on the far right of the stockroom counter."

Lillian left, and Levi gathered several boxes and gave them to Katie.

"CSNG24." He looked at Sadie. "Candles, small, no glass, and there are twenty-four of them, right?"

Sadie nodded. He was certainly smart enough to figure out her coding very quickly. What else had he figured out about her?

Levi slid another lightweight box onto Katie's stack. "Set these on the floor just inside the doorway to your left."

"Sure thing." Katie left.

Sadie's eyes met Levi's. "What have you been telling people?"

The muscles in his face went from relaxed to strained, but he didn't look at her.

"Nothing." He remained calm and steady as he sorted the boxes in stacks according to code.

Was he lying to her? Did Levi find it as easy to tell lies as Daniel had? That thought was disappointing at best and infuriating at worst.

The phone in his pocket buzzed. Short, loud, annoying rings. He pulled it out and glanced at the caller ID before sliding it back into his pocket.

Lillian and Katie returned, and he gave them each a stack with instructions and followed them into the store, carrying all but the last two boxes.

Sadie stood there, trying to make sense of who she'd thought Levi was compared to the man Lillian had just shoved in front of her face.

Lillian returned to the wagon. "Beth is writing up an invoice for you."

Sadie wasn't going to go inside the store right now. It was too much to pretend she was calm when she wanted to confront Levi. She put the last two boxes in Lillian's arms. "Tell her I need to go. We can settle up later. Okay?"

"You're sure?"

Right now, all she knew was that she needed to leave before she started an argument in front of everyone. "I'm sure. Denki."

Sadie climbed onto the bench of the wagon.

Levi strode back. "You're leaving already?"

"I'll ask you again. What have you been telling people?"

"Nothing." He shifted. "I mean, really, you know how people are."

This man right here, evading her questions and looking guilty, wasn't anything like the Levi she thought she knew.

"I think I'm beginning to understand how *you* are." With the reins in hand, she then realized she hadn't untied Bay from the post. "Do you mind untying my horse?"

His phone rang again. He ignored it this time and did as she asked. "What did Lillian and Katie say?"

"Oh, something about my being your girlfriend!"

A myriad of emotions crossed his face, beginning with surprise and ending with resignation. "Ya, about that... It's just people talking."

He had no idea how much she detested men who hid behind false behavior. It now tainted everything she'd thought or felt about Levi.

"Maybe you're new to how a woman would feel about what's happening here, so I'll clue you in. Honesty and an apology would be really wise moves about now. Anything less is just disappointing." She'd hoped to see a reflection of the true Levi in his countenance, but instead he seemed annoyed.

His jaw clenched. "I can admit I was wrong but not as bad as you're making it out to be. You're just doing the typical female thing. I saw Eva do that to my brother hundreds of times—make a mountain out of a molehill."

Once she'd asked about Andy's wife, and he'd said she was gone. What sort of man bad-mouthed someone who'd died? Did Sadie not know Levi any better than she'd known Daniel?

His phone buzzed again, and he simply stood there, staring at her as if they were strangers. Maybe they were.

"Would you answer that thing already?"

Levi pulled it from his pocket and pressed a button. "What?" He snapped the word out, and she startled. She'd never seen this side of him before. "He's here with the horses already?" Levi frowned and listened. "Okay, I'll be there soon." He said nothing for a moment. "I said *okay*." Levi disconnected the call and shoved the phone back into his pocket. "I need to go."

"Fine. Go." She tugged the right rein, steering Bay away from the hitching post. "Geh." Bay started toward the exit of the parking lot.

A few moments later Levi strode toward the horse's head and grabbed the leather cheeks of Bay's bridle, stopping her. His hand moved down the horse's neck, probably subconsciously assuring the animal she was safe. Animals he understood, but he studied Sadie as if disappointed in her.

Sadie's heart pounded. She'd thought they were friends, had been absolutely sure she liked who he was. Sometimes her ability to see what she wanted to see in someone astounded her. "So you have nothing to say to me?"

He shook his head. "I guess not."

"Geh!" She steered Bay out of the parking lot. Why had she ever come to Apple Ridge?

Fourteen

*L*evi could not believe himself. He watched as Sadie drove the rig from the parking lot and down the long road. Was he like an unreliable and high-strung horse that Sadie hated dealing with?

She'd been really good to him and was probably the sole reason his rescue included thorough medical help, the kind that ensured he took proper care of his injured neck. And he actually liked her. He respected who she was and admired her strength to politely stand against what their people expected of her.

He didn't know much else right now, but it was obvious he shouldn't have balked at what she'd demanded from him: an apology and honesty.

Jonah came up beside him with a clipboard filled with papers. "She left without stepping inside."

"Ya."

Levi had told himself to apologize to her. When he'd stopped her horse, he intended to tell her the truth. He'd wanted to say he was sorry. Instead, he'd just stood there. Whatever possessed him to use Sadie to make his life easier?

"Okay, here are the records for everything you brought in today." Jonah pulled copies of the receipts from the clipboard. "Should I give you Sadie's invoices too?"

"Probably not. If I tried to pass them on to her, she'd likely tear them up without looking to see what they are." Levi rolled up the receipts and swatted them against his leg. "I guess I messed up the meeting Sadie should've had with Beth."

"Businesswise, we can sort out everything with Sadie another day."

"Businesswise," Levi mumbled, watching Sadie's carriage disappear over a hill. "I don't think that'll help me at all."

Jonah stared at the horizon. "I don't know what happened, but I believe you are right about that."

Levi shoved the rolled-up papers into his pocket. "Apologizing to a woman doesn't come easy, does it?"

Jonah scratched the side of his face. "No, but it gets easier—for you and her."

Levi had never needed to apologize to a woman before, not really, certainly not like this. Oh, he'd apologized for some thoughtless incident at a church meeting or family gathering or such, for spilling a drink on a clean floor or nonsense like that. Those apologies came easy. The words flowed out of his mouth without his needing to think about them.

Apologizing to Sadie, though. That would've required him to make himself vulnerable. When he'd looked into her fiery eyes, it'd felt as if a team of wild horses couldn't have dragged the words out of him.

Levi debated whether to go home where work waited for him or to rush after Sadie. "This was my first argument with a girl. Not that I said much. But she sure said plenty."

Jonah chuckled. "Beth and I had our first argument the day she realized who I was. Long story, but I have to say you've nailed exactly how it went and how it felt. I think it's a female thing. They're usually more emotional than we are, and they've spent a lifetime trying to understand how they feel. They can think fast and argue with the past, present, and future in mind." He dug the bottom of his cane into the gravel. "If a couple cares for each other, though, you'll both learn to fight fair, and then you'll come away with a better understanding of her and yourself."

Levi stared at the storm clouds on the horizon. He wasn't interested in all that, but he did want to keep Sadie as a friend. He wanted letters from her when she was in the mission field. He wanted visits with her when she returned home. Twenty years from now, when they were both turning gray and their families had finally accepted who they were, he wanted to be on her to-visit list whenever she returned to the States.

"Jonah, I need to go. Tell Beth that I need to reschedule our meeting."

"Will do."

Levi untied his horse and climbed into his wagon. He soon pulled onto the main road, encouraging the horse to pick up speed. Even with his decision made, his chest had a weird heavy feeling to it. A kind of unfamiliar sadness.

But he wasn't sure why.

Maybe it was because of how he'd treated Sadie compared to what she deserved. Or maybe the sadness was because he knew he'd damaged her, and some part of him understood that they'd never get back the easy-flowing friendship they'd had.

⊂══⊃

Sadie ran wet towels through the wringer and dropped them into the clothesbasket. Why had her grandmother started a huge load of unsorted laundry while Sadie was at the store? on a Friday afternoon? Mondays were washdays, and Sadie didn't wash her dresses and undergarments with towels and black aprons.

She should never have come to Apple Ridge. The only reason she was here was to take a break from her parents. Well, that and she'd also needed to do some business with Beth.

And she'd wanted to see Levi.

What a mistake on every count. Clearly she'd put Levi on a pedestal. He'd seemed so nice, like a salt-of-the-earth person. How many times in life could she be fooled? How many times was she to feel this way...like an injured animal with nowhere to hide? December and the flight to South America could not come soon enough for her.

Mammi Lee pulled wet clothes out of the washer and put them into the clear water of the mud sink. "How you live isn't normal. You need to settle down, move back home permanently."

"I'm hoping that one day you'll accept that I'm not normal." She moved to the mud sink and plunged her hands on top of the soapy clothes, swishing them around. She pulled them out and plunged them again, not caring how wet she got. Her goal was to get this done and hang out the clothes by herself.

Mammi reached into the sink and pulled out a black apron. "You know the saying about bad apples? If Daniel was one, he doesn't ruin the whole barrel of them."

A knife plunged into Sadie's heart. "If?" She grabbed two handfuls of wet clothes from the sink and slung them into the basket. Forget running them through the wringer. She wanted out of this room. "So you're like everyone else and still stuck on *if* Daniel did what I said he did?"

Without saying a word, Mammi ran the black apron through the wringer.

Sadie picked up the basket and headed for the door. With her back against the door, about to push it open, she realized that Mammi was going to follow her. "I can do this by myself."

"I shouldn't have said 'if.' "

"But it's still what you think, isn't it?"

Mammi Lee pursed her lips, looking unsure. "I've never heard of an Amish man behaving like that. Not ever. But if you think that's what happened even all these years later, I tend to believe you saw it as you said."

That wasn't good enough, but Sadie wouldn't challenge her or anyone else on that topic. One couldn't make another believe. It was just that simple.

She drew a breath and stepped onto the front porch. Levi was at the hitching post, tying an unfamiliar horse. Of all the things she did *not* want to do, talking to him was at the top of her list.

Mammi stopped cold at the top of the steps, but Sadie descended, intending to ignore him.

"Afternoon, Verna," Levi called out. "I'd like to speak to your granddaughter for a few minutes if you don't mind."

"*I* mind," Sadie mumbled as she passed him on her way to the clothesline.

"It's mighty gut to see you again, Levi," Mammi spoke loudly. "You go right ahead, but she's testier than a yellow jacket in fall."

Levi fell into step with Sadie and leaned his head close to whisper to her. "That's the mood I've been in today. Maybe it's contagious."

"Go home, Levi."

"Come on, Sadie. Don't be like that. I know nothing about getting along with women. So cut me some slack."

She dropped the basket onto the ground and grabbed a dress out of it. It dripped, and she slung it, spraying water freely before pinning it to the line.

He glanced toward the house. "Could we maybe go for a walk or something?"

"No thank you, but please, by all means, go for a walk."

"So this is how you're going to be?"

"Pretty much."

He sighed and walked off. She didn't want him to go, yet she couldn't make herself do anything about it.

"Whoa!... Whoa!"

At Levi's holler, Sadie turned, then gasped. He was almost at her feet, flat on his back. Had he slipped on the wet grass? She knelt beside him. "Levi?"

He smiled. "You're nicer to me when I'm on my back and you think I'm injured."

"You faked that!" She got up, grabbed the basket of wet clothes, and dumped them on his face.

"Sadie!" Mammi yelled. "What has gotten into you?"

But he lay there, unmoving. "Denki."

She scoffed, trying to sound perturbed, but laughter stirred within her, and she cleared just enough wet clothing from around his eyes so he could see. "What is wrong with you?"

"I have a confession to make." His voice was muffled by the clothing.

She picked up most of the clothes and dumped them into the basket. "Doubt you can come up with one I haven't already figured out."

"Sadie!" Mammi sounded anxious.

Levi sat upright, picking a few more items of wet clothing off his chest and stomach. "It's my fault, Verna. Could you give me a few minutes to get it straight?"

Mammi pointed her finger at Sadie, giving a silent warning before going into the house.

Levi remained on the ground while he held the wet clothes out to

Sadie. When she took them, he hesitated about letting go. "I want to make things right between us."

"Ya, why?" She pulled the items free from him. "So you can start some other rumor of convenience behind my back when I leave?"

"Do you have to be ridiculous about this?" He stood, catching a last article or two of clothing that fell into his hands. "I came here to make it right. Isn't that enough?"

"*I'm* ridiculous? You're the one letting people think we're dating when you couldn't be bribed to ask me out."

"That's the stupidest thing I've ever heard. If you thought I wanted a date, you'd bar the door and hide under the bed." He held out the last item to her, and they both noticed it was a pair of her sky-blue lace underwear.

She jerked the underwear away from him. "You can't use the word *stupidest* when talking about how I feel."

"Okay, I promise not to use that word again. How about *dumbest,* most *blockheaded,* or *dimwitted*? Will those work for you?"

"Golly, you really *don't* know anything about getting along with women, do you?" She threw a wet towel in his face.

"No." He peeled it off. "But I know when I'm making progress, and you just hit me with one item instead of the whole basket."

Their eyes met, and she saw the same man who'd recognized her voice when she came to see him and had smiled before he opened his eyes. The same man who'd planted her feet in the path of an oncoming horse because he trusted she'd know what to do if need be.

She bent, picking some black stockings off the grass. "You shouldn't say disrespectful things about someone who's passed. We all make mistakes, and unlike us, they can't defend themselves or have one more day to try to make it right."

"I said something about a dead guy?"

"Eva! Remember?"

His eyes grew large. "*Ach,* ya, I do, but I didn't realize I'd said that. Look." He took the basket from her and set it to the side. "The subject of Eva is one I try not to think or talk about. I told you she's gone, and she is, but she packed her bags and left four years ago. That's when I moved in with Andy."

Eva wasn't dead? She'd abandoned her husband and son? That explained a lot. "And that's when you decided you'd never marry."

"It's a little more drawn out than that."

"It always is."

"If it helps, I never lied to anyone about you or us."

"Ya, it helps a lot." But that was it? He wasn't going to apologize?

She pinned a washrag to the clothesline, not at all sure she understood him, but the nice thing about being only friends was that she didn't have to. She could benefit from the enjoyable parts of their knowing each other and ignore the rest. That's what she'd done with her two roommates. "Katie said we're the buzz of the community. How'd that happen?"

"My guess is Mamm has been doing some hopeful whispering, and that with all the other connections Beth and Mattie know about—my getting your address and visiting you and our combining items to sell at the store—it just grew in people's minds."

"Why would your Mamm say anything?"

He explained about his parents being at his brother's house when he came back from her place with the boxes of crafts. The timing made it such that he couldn't hide where he'd been.

She secured a dress onto the line. "And since then we've been writing to each other, and I send letters and packages."

"Ya, and Tobias told my folks about the horse candle you made for me. All of it had Mamm so hopeful that I was seeing someone, and I couldn't tell her the truth."

"There's no way to keep that up for long. When were you going to tell them?"

"I don't know. Soon. But I went a few weeks with no one griping at me about not going to singings or needing a girl. It was really nice, but it was also selfish."

Maybe he was onto something. As long as Levi and Sadie knew where each stood, what could be wrong with people thinking they were dating? "It's not that I care whether people think we're dating or not."

"Wait. I'm confused. So what'd you get angry about?"

"I thought you had lied to me and about me."

"Oh, ya, I can see where that'd be angering."

She paused from hanging laundry and studied him. Did he know that hurt masqueraded as anger easily and often in a woman's heart? "It hurt, Levi. A lot."

Regret filled his eyes. "I'm truly sorry that I did anything to make you think I'd lie to or about you. I'd never do that."

Finally she had the heartfelt apology she'd wanted. And more. She believed in him again. "Forgiven." Ready to walk and talk, she left the clothes and went toward the dirt lane that meandered across the back field. Levi went with her.

"I think you were more selfish than you know." She poked his shoulder with her index finger. "You benefited from this, uh, misunderstanding. Why not let me?"

"I'm confused again."

"Maybe you don't need to set this straight with everyone. My parents are insisting I return home after I get my business with Hertzlers' squared away. It's so hard to be back there after living on my own for years. But they'd let me stay in Apple Ridge if we were courting. And Mammi Lee likes you, so she'd leave me alone about hiding from men. I could put all my focus on earning what I need to go with my mission team again."

"Isn't this too deceptive? I mean, not correcting someone's misconception is one thing, but to plot it out like this?"

"So we'll date. Look at us. We're a mess of distrust and not wanting to get involved with anyone. So if we were really dating, what are the chances of our staying together?"

"After what I just saw of us, I'd say zilch. You'd get hurt over something I didn't understand, and I'd find it impossible to apologize when you deserved it."

She knew he was here now only because of their friendship. If they were seeing each other romantically, they'd both have walked away today.

"Exactly. Besides, my parents say they believe in keeping the Amish ways and that I need to abide by them too, but according to the Old Ways, they're supposed to leave the matter of finding a mate in God's trustworthy hands, not their pushy ones. Right?"

"Ya, but I'm beginning to doubt the purity of your motives about mission work. Maybe you just don't want to cope with your parents' expectations."

"And you do?"

He grinned, looking like himself again. "You know the answer to that. So for how long?"

"We could break up a few weeks before I go to Peru. That would probably buy you six months to a year after I'm gone before people start pushing you to date again."

He looped his thumbs around his suspenders. "But if we're still courting when you leave, it'll be as if I'm waiting for you to return. That'll buy me a lot more time. A year. Maybe two years."

She turned onto the lane, and he joined her. "If we stay together and I try to leave on a mission trip, my Daed will go to the church leaders to keep me home. If he thinks I'm heartbroken, he'll let me go."

"Is that why they let you go the first time?"

"Ya, but I wasn't faking then. And going to Peru helped me heal in a way nothing else could have."

Levi nodded. He seemed to understand what heartache did to someone. "Eva shattered my brother's heart, and she ruined his life."

She'd had a pretty negative effect on Levi's life too. Did he realize that? "We've got three months to plan the timing of our relationship's demise." She leaned in, bumping his shoulder with hers. "There's something that's really important to me, okay?"

"It's okay with me if something is important to you."

She laughed and pushed against his shoulder again. "I'm not your mama or your girlfriend, so as we move forward, can we agree to be totally up-front with each other?"

"I believe I can do that."

"That includes no misdirecting me like your oddly worded statement that 'she's gone' or the like."

"Okay. But I've got one of those important things too."

"Let's hear it."

"I've already imagined us being friends and visiting each other even when we're old. Earlier today I thought I'd blown all chance of that."

She put her arm around his waist. "That's the best hope for a relationship I think I've ever heard."

"I'm glad you like it." He looped his arm around her shoulders. "Can we do it?"

She couldn't stop her grin. "I believe we can."

Fifteen

*L*evi fitted another piece of wood into place on the gazebo railing. The birch and maple trees around him swayed. Sadie said they were strutting their deep yellows and brilliant reds of fall like a peacock did his tail feathers.

He sighed. Girly nonsense. That's what she had him thinking these days. When he saw her in a bit, he'd complain about it too. He peered across the backyard and into his shop to check the clock again, then he hammered another nail into the railing. There was more work to do than he had morning left to do it.

Andy came around the corner of the house, two-by-fours stacked on top of one shoulder. Tobias was on his heels, carrying a two-by-two. Andy dropped his on the ground, and Tobias did the same. The planks banged and bounced, reminding Levi of the way sounds echoed through an empty home. Noise he wouldn't have noticed until these last few weeks with Sadie.

They used most of their courting time to work together on projects for the dry goods store. But when they weren't doing that, she liked to take long buggy rides and discover empty homes to walk through. It was an interesting pastime. Some of the places were new, unfinished homes that the builders abandoned when the economy changed. One home they went into was off by itself, a Victorian place. She loved that one best of all. Sadie's grandmother used to clean that house for the owners, a huge mansion Sadie had been in as a child. But the owners had passed away, and the house had yet to sell. She had few qualms about entering it, and even though the front door was locked, she'd found a side door that wasn't. When he'd balked, she said she knew the owners wouldn't have minded. If they were alive, she'd knock and visit with them, and she didn't care if the police showed up. He could hear her now: *"Let them take me to jail. I dare them."*

Just the thought made him laugh inside—a kind of hilarity he hadn't known until recently, where his outward expression showed little while inside he enjoyed great merriment.

They had yet to be caught breaking into a home. Although, if an officer or two did arrive, Levi would let Sadie do all the talking. She was the one who didn't mind defying authority as long as she wasn't doing any actual harm.

She was an odd bird, willing to bend her knee to whatever she thought God wanted of her and yet unwilling to yield to man's rules any more than absolutely necessary to stay out of serious trouble.

Levi had yet to fit those two women into one person—carefully defiant with a heart of utter obedience. Weird. The good news was that since they weren't really involved, he didn't have to be concerned about her attitude or outlook.

"Hello?" Andy set one of the boards on the sawhorses.

Levi looked up. "Did you say something?"

Andy turned to Tobias, shaking his head. Tobias clasped both hands to his head and moaned. The two kept telling him that lately he lived in a world of his own.

"I guess I was talking to myself." Andy brushed his hands together, knocking off the dust. "So what's today's game plan?"

Tobias jumped into the gazebo. "Ya, so what's going on tonight?"

Levi took a step back, looking at the clock inside his shop again. Did it need a new battery? It sure was moving slowly. "It's the annual hayride at Lizzy's, so I have about two hours before I pick up Sadie."

"Just two hours?" Tobias stomped across the gazebo, never looking up as he counted boards in some game he played.

"Ya." Levi pulled a nail from a pocket in his tool belt. "It's called a hayride, but it's an event for singles that starts right after lunch and lasts until midnight."

Tobias eyed him. "What'll you do all day?"

"Well, let's see. I've been told there'll be a cookout, volleyball and softball games, a hayride that'll last for at least an hour, a singing, and a bonfire."

Tobias shoved his hands into his pockets. "Why can't I go?"

"It's for singles."

Tobias rubbed his face, indicating he didn't have a beard. "I ain't married."

"You can't go, Son. It's for people at least sixteen years old." Andy pulled out a tape measure and put it against the two-by-four, his smirk undeniable. "Are you and Sadie staying at the gathering the whole time or coming by here after a while?"

"Don't know yet." Levi took a step back, inspecting his work. He shook the railing—steady as could be.

Tobias looked up, his eyes wide. "I hear something." He ran across the backyard and took off toward the front of the house.

Andy marked the wood with a pencil. "I can't believe Lizzy is still having those gatherings each year. I went to three before marrying, so my first time would've been twelve years ago."

Levi ran his hands across each nail, tapping certain ones a little deeper. "I've never been."

"Somebody your age and single shoulda been six or seven times by now. You do know Lizzy invites Amish from as far away as Illinois."

"Are you griping at me about girls again?"

"Sorry. Old habits die hard, I guess."

Tobias came around the corner of the shop. "Sadie's here."

"She is?" Levi left the gazebo, a smile tugging at his lips.

Tobias hurried back along with him.

Sadie had some craft items spread out in his shop, so maybe she needed something from her stash. Sometimes she worked here when there was no more shelf space at Mammi Lee's. It took quite a bit of room when juggling wreaths, candles, soaps, and dolls during the same workweek.

She came into view, wearing a purple dress and carrying a large basket lined with red fabric. Tobias was in front of her, walking backward and jabbering.

Levi spun his hammer around a few times, making the head of it rotate similar to a helicopter. "Is it soup yet?"

She'd made a batch of soap a couple of days ago that came out the consistency of soup—and he hadn't stopped harassing her about it yet.

Her eyes moved from Tobias to him. "Leave me alone, Fisher."

The way she talked—those firm words spoken dryly—made him chuckle. It was her best effort to sound tough despite teasing, and he knew she'd dish out equal amounts of whatever pestering he came up with.

He shoved his hammer into its loop on his tool belt and took the basket from her. "Or what? You'll wash my mouth out with soup...I mean soap?"

She pursed her lips, looking peaceful and sweet as he harassed her, but he knew she wouldn't just leave it at a smile. There would be a price to pay.

"Excuse me?" Levi leaned in, cupping one hand behind his ear. "What was that you said, Sadie Yoder?"

Sadie flashed him a mocking look of anger before spotting his brother. "Hey, Andy, how are you?"

Andy nodded, giving a welcoming smile as he remained at the sawhorse. "Morning, Sadie."

She pointed at the gazebo. "It's looking good. I suppose that means you managed to make Levi use a straightedge and a level."

"Of course." Andy winked at Tobias. "It's standing straight, ain't it?"

"Hey." Levi waved an arm. "I'm right here as you insult me."

She eyed him from head to foot. "With a tool belt, a girly basket in your hands, and doing absolutely nothing."

"Sadie." Tobias looked up, eyes bright with questions. "Can we sit on the fence and watch Levi work with the horses again?"

She glanced at Levi before clearing her throat. "He needs us to give him some lip while he's training, doesn't he?"

Tobias grinned. "I think so."

"I don't agree." Levi shrugged, but he actually enjoyed their harassment while he worked.

"Tobias, give me a hand." Andy held out a pencil, probably aiming to keep him distracted so Sadie and Levi could talk.

Levi opened the screen door to the workshop, and Sadie went in ahead of him. She took the basket and unloaded dried flowers, wire, and half-made wreaths.

"Lizzy asked me to bring centerpieces for the tables at the cookout, and I've cleaned Mammi's small patch of woods for other projects." She picked up her now-empty basket. "You can go on working while I hunt for flowers."

"Me, do woodwork when I can pick flowers?" He opened the door again. "No way." He could make up next week for taking off early today. Besides, he'd worked long, hard hours six days a week for years. Sadie was here for only two more months, so he had no problem taking off when it suited him.

They headed for a trail that hadn't been all that familiar to him before he'd started helping Sadie gather items for her wreaths. Now that she lived closer to Hertzlers', she was able to fill orders quickly and get them to the store without cost or delay. She was making great money.

"Uncle Levi?"

Andy shushed his son, but Sadie bumped her shoulder into Levi's. "Let the boy come with us."

Levi turned, motioning for him.

Andy angled a look at them. "You sure?"

"We're sure."

Tobias thundered past them. "I bet I can find the best flowers again."

They went deeper in the woods, leaving the trail at will and quipping nonsense at each other as they found treasures for the wreaths.

"Tobias," Sadie called, "kumm." She pointed to a patch of Johnny-jump-ups. Tobias headed their way.

Basket in hand, Sadie straddled a log, aiming to get what was on the other side.

Levi leaned against a tree, keeping an eye on Tobias as he made his way to Sadie. When Tobias passed him, Levi bumped the hat off his head.

"Uncle Levi!" Tobias bent to grab it.

Sadie screamed an ear-piercing shrill.

Levi bolted upright, but he was sure he knew what the problem was.

"It's something furry!" She hopped and danced before jumping up on the log. She shook her arms before gasping. Apparently she'd seen the culprit afresh. And a blur of purple hurtled toward him.

Before Levi could react, she jumped into his arms. "Ew, yuck!" She shuddered against him.

He didn't know what to do or say. While seeing a critter out here wasn't new, and it always caused her to immediately panic, Sadie jumping into his arms was a first.

A mouse ran out from under the log, and Levi laughed so hard it was difficult not to fall over backward.

"It's not funny!" Sadie smacked him with the flat of her fist. "Geh." She shooed the creature away as if it could see her antics from deep in the brush.

"I fear I'd be dead if a mouse had scurried out at any point that night I was thrown from my horse."

She studied the ground. "Where'd it go?"

He winked at Tobias and began searching around while holding her. "I don't know...wait, it's on my shoe." He kicked one foot up.

Sadie fled from his arms and didn't stop until she was on the log. "Where?"

Levi couldn't stop laughing. He didn't know which was funnier: the color of Tobias's face as he chortled or the look of terror on Sadie's face as she searched for the tiny, furry creature.

She pointed at him. "I'll get you for that, Fisher."

"I doubt you can top that, Sadie."

But he couldn't deny he looked forward to her trying. They had two months to go. Plenty of time for her to plot against him.

And for him to foil her plans each time.

Sixteen

Jonah stretched and reached across the bed for his wife. When he felt only air, he rubbed his hands across the sheets. Cold. Not only was she missing, she'd been gone for a while. He opened his eyes. Rays of golden light streamed through the windows.

He pushed back the thermal blanket and quilt and sat up. The room was unusually warm for late November. Had Beth been up toting wood and stoking fires while he slept? On a Sunday morning?

He slid into his pants and house shoes, pulled the suspenders over his shoulders, and grabbed his cane. His bad leg yelped in pain as he hurried down the hall without giving the muscles time to warm up. While passing the potbellied stove in the living room, he held out his hand. Heat radiated from it. That wasn't the only thing in this house that had an internal fire licking at it.

He and Beth had argued more than once about this. The last time occurred a couple of months ago when he'd walked into the store after hours and seen her at the top of a six-foot ladder getting something off a shelf. That explosion had been a real barnburner, but he'd won. Or so he'd thought.

Walking through the sitting room, he saw a roaring fire in the hearth.

"Beth!" Where was she? They had an agreement—no climbing ladders and no toting anything heavy. "Beth!"

Through the french doors a flash of patchwork caught his eye. She stood at the railing on the porch, a quilt wrapped around her as she studied the fields. He grabbed his coat from the rack and went outside.

She turned—steam rising from a mug of dark liquid in her hands. Her raven hair was in a long braid that draped down one shoulder. Her blue eyes were filled with peace and love. "Good morning."

Good morning? Was she kidding? "You should've woken me."

Her smile toyed with his emotions. She deserved his wrath.

"Look." She nodded toward the west. Low-hanging gray clouds hovered on the horizon. "I think we may see the first snow flurries of the year today." He knew she loved snow and all it symbolized, the things that had gone on between them. The fallen tree he'd dragged through the snow and up a ravine before he even knew her. He'd used it to carve a scene on a large base, one she'd stumbled upon in a store, and it'd called to her. It was the reason they'd eventually met. Snow reminded her of the storm he'd rescued her from in the sleigh he'd refurbished for her.

Despite the memories he held firm to his anger. "I'm not pleased right now."

She smiled. "Your little one is leaping for joy this morning. I think he or she senses the beauty of today." She opened one edge of her blanket, inviting him to place his hand on her round belly.

He sighed and set his cane aside before stepping up behind her. He wrapped his arms around her and placed one hand inside her quilt. The baby jolted numerous times, kicking or punching as if playing a game. "What am I going to do with you, Beth Hertzler Kinsinger?" The scent of lavender clung to her skin, and he kissed her neck.

"I don't know." She angled her head, inviting more kisses. "Love me? Create a family with me?"

"Attach bells to you."

She laughed. "Do what?"

"You've been good lately, well behaved as long as I'm on my feet, keeping an eye on you. Bells will give me a way to know when you get up."

"Ah. I see." She placed her hand on his as it pressed against her stomach. "Just make sure they're sleigh bells, and I won't mind too much."

He tugged her, and she faced him. He put his forehead against hers. "Please."

"Not even firewood to warm our home for you?"

"Not even."

"You do know you're being ridiculous and demanding—two things I did not expect from you when we married."

He cradled her face, still mesmerized by all God had done in bringing them together. "I'd gladly strike a match and burn down our home, the business, and every item we possess if it meant I could keep you even a little safer."

"That's a bit drastic, don't you think?"

"What I think is that you don't understand. You mean everything to me, and we're expecting something that cannot be replaced."

"It's a between Sunday, and I wanted to let you sleep."

"So your desire for me to get extra sleep matters more than following what your husband feels is important?"

Her eyes filled with tears. "Not when you put it that way."

It wasn't like her to be emotional, and he knew she struggled at times with the hormones coursing through her body.

She shrugged. "I don't believe it's necessary to be that pampered, but I'll not tote another thing."

"Gut." He moved his lips to hers, and their kiss lingered. He then stared into her eyes. "Extremely warm outside to be after Thanksgiving, ya?"

She giggled.

He opened the door for her to go inside. "So what has you up and moving like this on our off Sunday?"

"You know." She took off the quilt and laid it across the back of a kitchen chair. "The indoor picnic Mattie and I planned."

Jonah took the mug of coffee from her hands and took a sip. "But that's not until this afternoon."

"Life is too exciting right now to sleep." She put her hand on her round belly.

For a moment Jonah saw a tiny bit of what his wife was feeling. Their child's first steps, first day at school, and first time to ride a horse. It would all take place in the blink of an eye, and he understood her need to soak in the moments.

But for all the excitement that radiated from her, he couldn't shake the uneasy feeling nagging at him.

Nippy air and the familiar aromas of a barn—sweet feed, hay, and animals in wintry weather—surrounded Sadie as she removed the rigging that connected Bay to the carriage.

Mammi went to the bag of feed and scooped up the dry mixture. "We heard three good sermons today, ya?"

Church had been at the Ebersol place today, which was where she and Mammi Lee had been since morning. It'd be dark in an hour. Between the three-hour meeting, the after-church meal, and the long afternoon of fellowshipping, Sadie had been gone all day.

"I'm sure the preachers touched many a heart." But the truth was, Sadie hadn't heard much of what'd been said. Then as now, her mind lingered elsewhere. Thoughts of Levi drifted through her nonstop. Reflections of him—their many dates, hundreds of conversations, working side by side to make items for the dry goods store, visits with family and friends—all of it seemed to remain uncomfortably close.

Mammi's gait was slow and steady as she walked to the stall where Sadie would lead Bay in a few minutes. Mammi spread the feed into the trough. "Seems to me like you oughta attend a few Sunday meetings in Levi's district soon."

Sadie moved slower than her grandmother as she slid the bridle off Bay and attached a loose-fitting harness. Her muscles seemed as distracted as her heart. It was a between Sunday for Levi's district, and although they spent a lot of time together, they didn't attend meetings with each other. She wasn't sure why. "He hasn't asked me to."

Mammi shuffled across the hard-packed dirt, collecting pieces of straw on the wide rim of her flat black shoes as she went. "But you two are going to tonight's singing, right?"

She shook her head. "Not this time."

"Why?" Mammi jammed the scoop into the dry feed and dusted off her gloved hands.

Sadie wasn't sure about that either—except maybe she and Levi both knew they'd grown too close. "I don't know." They'd been dating and almost inseparable for twelve weeks. Their time together would be up in a month. Maybe he was laying the foundation for folks to believe they were having trouble.

But she wasn't ready.

She'd let her guard down with Levi, and she believed he'd done the same with her. He'd gotten under her skin, and she didn't know how to free herself of him. Or even if she wanted to.

Mammi rested her hand on Sadie's shoulder. "Everything okay between you two?"

Tears pricked Sadie's eyes. "Ya. I…I hope so." Weeks ago if Mammi had asked that, Sadie would have probably given the same answer, only then it would have been part of the show she and Levi were putting on.

The soft wrinkles around Mammi's eyes creased. Her smile held confidence in the situation. "I'm sure how he feels. I see it in his eyes."

Did Mammi really?

That was comforting.

And terrifying.

"You coming?" Mammi headed for the small door at the back of the barn. They'd already struggled through closing the double-wide door to keep out the cold.

"In a bit." Sadie stroked Bay's forehead and face, trying to sense what Levi sensed when training horses. It was as if he became one with the animal, seeing and feeling what the horse did, and then worked with the massive creature from its peculiarities and personality.

Closing her eyes, she let her fingertips caress Bay's neck. The mare's skin radiated warmth and quivered under Sadie's light touch. What must a saddle feel like to one that responded to such a feathery stroke?

In Sadie's mind, she could see Levi working a horse and hear his gentle commands. The features on his face altered ever so slightly, and she'd learned which tiny shift in expression meant he was perplexed or pleased or any of the other dozens of emotions that ran through him while training.

Someone cleared his throat, and she opened her eyes. Levi stood a few feet away, his black felt hat matching his winter coat as he studied her with quiet curiosity.

Her heart beat faster, but words failed her.

He moved in closer and placed his hands on the horse's neck. "If this was your first time getting to know the horse, you'd have to let go of your will." He drew a deep breath. "Relax, Sadie." He put his cold hand over hers. "It's not about what you want from the horse. Release your expectations. Your preconceived ideas."

The seconds ticked by.

"When I'm with a horse,"—Levi moved his fingertips across the back of her hand as if willing her to feel the horse's heart—"I have to set aside what the buyer has told me or what he hopes to gain. Let nothing get between you and simply accepting this creature for who she is."

Sadie inhaled and exhaled, trying to free her mind so she could sense what the horse felt. Levi's hand was warm now, his breathing less smooth than when he'd arrived. He wanted something, longed for—

She opened her eyes. "I think Bay is hungry and would like to go to bed for the night."

Levi shook his head. "Tobias could've come up with that at two years old. Clear your mind."

"I did."

"And?"

She eased away from him and grabbed a brush. "I thought we agreed that we weren't seeing each other today?" Running the brush down Bay's side, Sadie willed herself not to look up. But she did anyway.

Levi stared at her, seemingly wanting an answer to his question. "We received an invitation a few days ago from Beth and Jonah."

"Ya?" She placed the bristles on Bay's side. "Then you had the invitation when you suggested we not see each other. Didn't you?"

He shrugged. Did he miss her like she missed him?

He looked at the palm of his hand, the one that had been over hers moments ago. "They had an indoor picnic at their home earlier today.

With the exception of you, everyone is in the same church district, so they didn't have a service today. Gideon and Mattie, Lizzy and Omar, Annie and Aden."

"Who are Annie and Aden?"

"You met them once when we were making a delivery to Hertzlers'. He's Old Order Amish, and she was Old Order Mennonite, but she's in the process of joining our faith."

"I don't remember meeting them. Old Order Mennonites can have electricity. Why would she take a step into a harder life?"

"Because they fell in love, and she wants to be a part of his family, his church, and his business."

His words made her mouth and throat go dry. "Oh."

Levi drew a deep breath. "Omar, our bishop, has a lot of love for people, and as a bishop he can make it easy and appealing for people to return if they've left Apple Ridge or to join their loved ones here to build a life, like Jonah did with Beth."

She heard his words, but after he said "fell in love," she couldn't pay much attention. Running the brush down Bay's side again and again, she held her tongue, afraid her voice would betray her.

"We've missed most of it." Levi fidgeted with Bay's mane. "But if we go, the gathering will only include five couples. They had an indoor picnic earlier, but tonight they'll roast marshmallows inside, drink apple cider, and play board games."

She moved to the far side of Bay, staying focused on the short red hairs flying as she brushed the horse. What kind of people pretended to be a couple to those they cared about?

Or were she and Levi only pretending to each other?

"I guess." Emotions caught in her throat again, and she turned her back to him and walked to the weathered barn wall where she laid the brush on a chest-high beam. When she turned, Levi was directly in front of her.

There it was again—that feeling of him wanting something. Hadn't she sensed this same thing in him for weeks now? She could ask him about it, but as she looked into his eyes, she knew the answer.

And he wasn't the only one who'd like to stop their pretend courtship long enough to share a very real kiss.

Go around him, Sadie. But she stood there, feet planted, staring up at him like a schoolgirl. "What have we done, Levi?"

"I wish I knew." He sounded as confused as she felt, but he brought one hand to her face and caressed it. "Still, I think any courtship that's lasted three months should include one kiss."

Her heart turned a flip, wanting the same thing he did. From what he'd told her, it'd be his first kiss.

He looked at her face where his fingers barely touched her skin. "Seems like when I'm gray, this old bachelor should at least know what it's like to put his lips against yours."

His words were a mix of keeping up their pretense and letting it slip that he didn't want to experience just any kiss. He wanted to kiss her.

Is this who they were, only able to share their hearts when pretending they weren't?

"Seems like." She let her response continue their stupid charade, too afraid to let him know that somewhere along the way over the past three months, she'd crossed over from their faux nonsense into truly caring.

He lowered his mouth to hers. Stiffness greeted her lips, sort of like being kissed by a warm rock.

"Relax, Levi." She tugged on the collar of his coat. "Release your expectations and preconceived ideas. Let nothing get between us."

He moved his lips over hers again, and in one shared breath, her guard—and his—melted. His arms tightened around her, and as she let herself be lost in his embrace, she pushed away the question clamoring at her heart and mind…

How would she ever again convince herself that what they had was only make-believe?

Seventeen

B eth leaned over her desk and jotted down more notes for the morning meeting. In the distance a rooster crowed over and over, grating
on her nerves. It'd begun its nonsense thirty minutes before sunrise, and
it'd been daylight for about that long too. Wishing it'd stop, she opened
a drawer and pulled out a file.

Her abdomen contracted again. Braxton Hicks contractions. That's
what the midwife had called them. It was a sort of false labor the body
used as it geared up for the real thing.

She glanced at the clock on her office wall, waiting for her muscles to
relax. The night had been a long one because the tightness awakened her
at least once an hour. Were the contractions getting harder?

Someone tapped on her office door, and before she had enough air
to respond, Jonah opened it. "Everyone's here, and we've cleared enough
space for a circle of twenty chairs. You ready?"

"Soon."

"Would you like a cinnamon roll?"

"No, denki." Another contraction made her heart rate go wild. It was
just December 10. How many more weeks needed to pass before she'd be
full term? Maybe she'd calculated wrong.

Holding that hope, she forced a smile and began gathering her
papers. "I'll be right there."

He winked and closed the door, and she swiped the papers and folders off her desk calendar. Today was December 10. The doctor set her due date as January 21.

Maybe he was wrong. But what if he wasn't?

She pulled air into her lungs, wishing she could get a full breath.

"Beth?" Jonah called.

She grabbed a red pen and circled the date on her calendar, counting the days until she'd be full term. The midwife said there was a difference between premature and preterm—a vitally important difference. What had she explained? The pen squeaked as Beth marked each day. She'd be full term December 31. That was…nineteen, twenty, twenty-one days from now.

Could their child survive if born this early? She wiped perspiration from her forehead. *Look at what you're doing to yourself, Beth. They're Braxton Hicks, and you've got yourself all keyed up over it.*

"Beth." Jonah opened the door. His eyes moved to the papers in the floor, the pen in her hand, and the red marks on the calendar.

She smiled. "Sorry. I'm getting clumsier with each passing day."

"Not a problem." He picked up the mess, sorting out her meeting notes from the invoices.

She peered out the door.

With the exception of her and Jonah and Mattie and her husband, Gideon, everyone else attending was an employee.

Gideon stood next to Mattie, one hand on her back as they talked with Lillian. Gideon's eyes reflected such joy, and he looked vibrant and strong. He'd been given another clean bill of health a few weeks back. There was no trace of the rare cancer that had tried to destroy him. Mattie's return to Apple Ridge had allowed Gideon and her to face the truth that they loved each other enough to face an uncertain future together.

Beth thought about Levi. He wasn't here, but he'd been out of his neck brace for a few weeks now, another tale of woe turned into triumph. She could remember trials and triumphs in the life of almost everyone she knew.

Still, her heart beat faster and faster. Surely she and Jonah would have a triumph too. In fact, a beautiful little triumph to cherish for the rest of their days. But one common thread ran through each victory: no one had ignored their symptoms while hoping for the best.

She laid the pen on her desk. "Jonah, honey."

He looked up from the mess of papers on the floor, and the confidence in his eyes turned to concern. "Something wrong?"

She shrugged. "I'm not sure."

He moved toward her. "Do you need to be seen?"

"Probably not." She hated to cause the worry she saw in Jonah's eyes. "But maybe we—" Suddenly Beth felt a jolt, as if the baby was sideways. Another contraction tightened across her stomach, stealing her breath. She clutched Jonah's hand.

He grabbed the phone. "I'm calling the midwife."

A gust of frigid air thrashed against Levi as he left the barn, leading the last horse toward Daniel's trailer.

Daniel had pen in hand and a forearm planted firmly on the papers piled on the hood of the truck. "She's number twenty-six fourteen, right?"

Tip sat inside the cab, talking on his cell phone.

"Technically,"—Levi patted the mare's strong cheek—"her name is Angel."

Like nearly everything in his life these days, she was a source of memories that connected Levi to Sadie. Tobias and Sadie had sat on a fence while Levi worked with Angel, and they'd each ridden her, helping him make sure the horse listened to women and children almost as easily as she listened to him.

He directed Angel up the ramp and into the trailer and closed the gate. One more task accomplished, and that meant he was one step closer to his date tonight with Sadie—an evening he hoped would change both of their futures.

After their kiss six days ago, he could no longer ignore the truth: he loved her. He couldn't let her leave without telling her how he felt. Sure, her plans were in place, but he could wait for her to return. Why not wait? It wasn't as if he was giving up anything—except time with her. He could wait.

That night, after the kiss, they'd gone to Beth and Jonah's. The evening of parlor games and fellowship had been a lot of fun, but he'd spent most of the time trying to figure out what to say to Sadie. On the way home, he'd told her to think about what she really wanted from their relationship and he'd do the same, and they'd talk about it next week.

Levi moved to the front of the truck. Daniel held up some papers and motioned to Tip, who was still on the phone behind the wheel.

Tip ended his phone conversation and got out. "I think we've got three of the four horses placed already. There's a man a hundred and fifty miles north of here who wants to see them. If he agrees they're all I told him they are, we'll get top dollar."

"Good." Daniel passed him the papers. "You know what to do."

Tip headed for the house. Andy handled the business end of Daniel's arrangements with the Fisher brothers.

Levi was headed inside to get warm and have some breakfast, but Daniel wanted to talk. He leaned against the truck cab and pulled a pack of gum from his coat pocket. "You're raking in a lot of dough off these horses lately, aren't you?"

Levi chuckled. "We aren't doing bad, me and you."

"Not bad? I'd say that's how we've been doing the past few years. But since being thrown from Amigo, you seem to have figured out the key to taming horses." He held out the pack to Levi.

Levi took a stick and put it in his pocket for later. He wasn't much for chewing gum, but Sadie liked it. He hoped that, after her week of thinking about their upcoming conversation, she'd accept how he felt. He'd certainly count that as a step in the right direction, but it'd be the night of his life if she actually had feelings for him too.

Daniel played with the foil wrapper, straightening it and flipping it. "It'll take me and Tip most of the day to make our deliveries, but we'll be back to pick you up if you want to go to the auction tonight."

"I have other plans."

"What?" Daniel's brows arched. "This seems to be a regular occurrence of late. Are you seriously seeing somebody?"

"I hope so... I mean, we haven't talked about how we feel or where we're going."

Daniel poked his shoulder, grinning. "I'll tell you how to feel—like your tail's on fire and you should run for the hills."

"I got plenty of that going on." Levi needed no encouragement when it came to wanting to run from relationships. But Sadie was different. "We met in July, so I think I'm getting to know her pretty well."

"Are you tellin' me this is the same girl you dumped me for in August?"

"I showed up at the auction."

"Ya, hours late and completely spent."

"Ya, it's the same girl."

"Really?" Daniel angled his head, apparently confused by Levi's change of heart. "You need a ride into Stone Creek again?"

Levi chuckled. "You're behind the times. She's living in Apple Ridge with her grandmother."

"You haven't talked about her much."

What could Levi say? He was pretending to court a girl and got caught in a very real snare?

Daniel crossed his arms, his breath a white vapor as he chewed his gum. "I guess it was bound to happen. You thinking about turning in your bachelor's license?"

"Thinking about it—if there is such a thing."

Daniel rolled his eyes. "You're playing a dangerous game, man. You'll be in love one minute and daydreaming of her demise the next. All the while she'll be stacking the deck against you, and you won't even know it."

"Sadie's not like that."

"I believe you. You've got a knack for seeing into horses. I'm sure that works on females too." Daniel chuckled. "Although you can clearly be wrong about horses, or you wouldn't have been riding one that overreacts to fireworks on the Fourth of July."

Daniel's aim was humor, but Levi didn't find anything humorous about what he'd said.

"It's sort of an odd coincidence." Daniel pulled his coat collar up high, shielding his neck from the wind. "That girl I was engaged to, she was a Sadie too." He sighed, shaking his head. "Messed up my life." He waggled a couple of fingers near the side of his forehead. "Did a real tap dance inside my brain." He stood upright.

Levi began to walk toward the house, ready to get out of the cold. Daniel followed him.

"Ya, I'm well aware that a woman can do that. I saw it happen to Andy, and I imagine Sadie could do it to me."

Daniel tossed the wrapper on the ground. "You say she's living near here?"

"Ya, her folks are from Brim, but she's living with her grandmother."

Daniel stopped, his eyes wide. "Tell me her grandmother isn't Verna Lee and her name isn't Sadie Yoder."

"How'd you—" Levi's worst fears swarmed like locusts and devoured every hope he'd imagined. His Sadie was the same girl who'd broken up with Daniel the day before their wedding? The thought of her courting Daniel, of her growing close to him the way she had with Levi sickened him. Worse, she'd run out on Daniel—just as Eva had done to Andy.

"It's your life, Levi. Maybe she's changed." He pulled the gum from his mouth and threw it into the bushes. "But years ago she was sweeter than candy and eventually showed me a side that was battier than bats. My concern is that, given time, she'll find some excuse and leave you like she did me." He went to the front door and paused. "Has she said anything about me?"

"Not a word."

He seemed relieved. "If you talk to her about this, she'll tell you I was to blame. But it was the day before our wedding, and I just happened to be in a room alone with one of her cousins. Sadie walked in. Maybe she actually thinks she saw something. I don't know. But I believe she was looking to bolt, and making up lies about what she saw was her way out."

Levi could easily imagine Sadie getting cold feet and wanting to run.

Even so, he loved her. Every goofy, funny, charming thing about her. How was it possible that he'd fallen for the same woman as Daniel? He hadn't been clear on who Daniel's fiancée was, but if he had, there were five Sadie Yoders that he knew of in the district. Since Daniel was a bit of a nomad, he'd lived in numerous Amish communities, and Levi imagined Daniel knew at least twenty Sadie Yoders.

Realization almost pounded him to the ground. He'd fallen for the same kind of woman as his brother had: a woman who hooked a man and then changed her mind about loving him.

God, why? He'd thought God was leading him *out* of the wilderness.

His thoughts came in disjointed fragments. All his senses seemed to heighten as his dream world shattered, causing him to see his reality for what it was.

Around him, the empty limbs of trees shook in the wind, and a few brown leaves tumbled across the dead grass—both evidence of the arrival of another long season of barrenness.

The horses he'd spent months training would be sold later today, becoming no more to him than a way to make money.

The woman he loved was incapable of building a life with anyone, banishing him to a life of isolation.

And Levi had to face yet another truth: he was a fool.

But he wouldn't stay that way.

He turned, seeing Daniel still standing at the back door, waiting in the cold for Levi to get a grip on himself.

Levi drew a heavy breath. The first of many, he imagined. "I've changed my mind. I will go with you tonight after all."

Eighteen

The horse's hoofs kept rhythm against the pavement, the familiar *clippity-clop* not moving swiftly enough for Sadie's liking. A muddled gray daylight had edged over the top of the mountain a little while ago. Snow flurries swirled, dancing on air, as the horse and carriage joggled its way down the road.

She shouldn't be on her way to Levi's on a Sunday morning. It seemed self-indulgent to *have* to talk to him first thing on the Sabbath. It was God's day, not hers. Still, she tugged on the left rein, turning the carriage onto Hertzler Drive.

What was going through Levi's mind? He'd made it very clear they needed to use the week to think about what they wanted. They were supposed to go out last night to talk, but then he left a message on the machine in Mammi's phone shanty. He said he wouldn't be coming by to pick her up and that he thought it best if they continued to follow their original plan.

What?

She'd been having second thoughts about meeting up with her mission team and leaving the country. How could she leave when she'd fallen in love with Levi Fisher? She had no doubt about that. So the only question was what God would have her do now: keep her plans to return to the mission field in Peru or stay here.

Levi had to be feeling the same things she felt. Both of them were terrified of making a commitment. But they were different together than she and Daniel had been. She imagined they were different than Andy and Eva had been.

She and Levi were strong enough to let go of their fears and love each other. She'd spent a week praying about it, after which she found that she had no reservations about Levi. But what would it take to convince him? Maybe he *needed* her to leave. Maybe they needed to spend a year writing to each other.

Sadie slowed the rig, preparing to enter Levi's driveway. It looked as if a lamp was lit in the kitchen. Gut. Maybe she wouldn't need to wake the house to get someone to the door. After tying the horse to the hitching post, she went to the front door and tapped on the glass.

Andy came into view, mug in hand. He smiled and opened the door. "Sadie. Kumm, get in out of the cold."

She stepped inside, and he closed the door behind her.

"You going to church with us this morning?"

"No." The aroma of coffee permeated the air, but there wasn't a sound anywhere else, as if even the house itself were still asleep. "Is Levi up?"

"Don't think so, but I can fix that for you." He set his mug on the table. "Take off your coat and make yourself at home. He was at the auction until late, so it may take me a bit to rouse him. Would you like a cup of coffee while I get him?"

"No, denki." She didn't know if she'd be here long enough to drink it, but she removed her coat and hung it on the back of a kitchen chair. "I'm fine."

Andy disappeared down the hall. She liked the way he treated her, as if he had a quiet hope of who she and Levi would become. He seemed to love his brother as much as he did his son. Despite his situation, Andy acted as if he believed in marriage. Why had his wife left him? He seemed pleasant and even-keeled—traits that could make a marriage work even if two people fell out of love.

Had he been unfaithful to her, so she just left? Sadie detested that she'd even thought such a horrid thing, but since she'd discovered Daniel with Aquilla…well, such thoughts came to her far more often than she liked to admit.

Andy returned, a smile on his face. "He jolted up the second I opened the door." He went to the stove and poured a little more black liquid into his half-full mug. "Any snow sticking to the roads yet?"

"Not yet." She wanted to ask him how Levi felt about her. If anyone knew, Andy would. But it wouldn't be right to do so. Levi had the right to insist he and Sadie stick to their original plan and break up regardless of any fondness he had for her.

He did care for her…didn't he?

"That's good, although I'm sure Tobias would love for enough snow so we could miss a church day. I imagine Levi and the two other guys who stayed over last night might be tempted to want the same. I don't think they crawled into bed until around four." Andy took a sip of his drink. "I was about to start breakfast. Will you stay and eat with us?"

"She won't be able to stay."

Levi's hard words sliced at her heart, and she turned.

He fastened the last button on his shirt and pointed at her coat. "Let's go outside."

"It's freezing out there." Andy set his cup on the table. "Everyone else is asleep. I'll go to my room."

Levi grabbed his coat off a peg. "It'll be warm enough in the barn."

She didn't move to get her coat, and a glance at Andy indicated she wasn't the only one baffled by Levi's attitude.

"It was good to see you, Sadie." Andy nodded and left the room.

Sadie put her hands on her coat, not quite ready to do as Levi had instructed.

"You broke our date rather last minute yesterday, and then you were out all night. Now I don't even get a hello, and you can't get me out of the house quickly enough. If I didn't know better, I'd say you had a girl you were hiding."

A look flashed through his eyes—disappointment in her, maybe. But why?

He reached over and picked up her coat. "We began our relationship as one thing, and it turned into another. We both know that's true. I think a clean break is best. Our breakup was supposed to be inevitable, so we'll let it begin today."

He held the coat out to her, waiting for her to slip into the sleeves.

Concern niggled at her, and she brushed hair away from his face. "Did you hit your head or something? You don't look or sound like the man I've come to know these last three months."

He didn't pull away, but the rigid look on his face said he wanted to. "Look, Sadie, you've been amazing from the start. And I know I owe you more than I can ever repay, but—"

"*Owe* me?" She backed up, staring at him. Had he mistaken gratitude for true caring? "All you feel for me is tied to my helping you that night?"

"Don't do this, Sadie."

"Do what? Try to understand?"

He said nothing.

She couldn't catch her breath, and her suddenly weak knees plunked her into a kitchen chair. "Maybe you're just spooked. Have we moved too fast? Because I could keep my missions plans. We could write to each other, and maybe by the time my work is finished, you'd feel ready to—"

"No." He hooked her coat on one finger and held it out. "I won't."

Tears stung her eyes, and she rose. "So this is it?"

He looked at the floor before meeting her eyes. "If it helps, I'm not happy about how things turned out either."

A door somewhere down the hall opened. It was probably Tobias.

Levi clutched the doorknob. "Kumm, I'll walk you to your carriage."

She put on her coat. "No, I'm fine." She paused in front of him. "When you asked me to spend a week thinking about where I wanted us to land, I thought…I mean, you sounded…"

His eyes locked on hers. "I know, and I'm sorry it has to be this way."

"Ya, me too." She choked back tears. "But it is what we agreed to."

He started to open the door, and she placed her hand in front of it. "Jonah was trying to reach you yesterday. He called Mammi Lee's looking for you. I didn't talk to him, only listened to the message, but he'd like for you to come by today when you can."

"I left my phone here last night."

"You, without your phone?" Her mind spun. People were seldom good at being direct, but their actions often told everything that needed to be said. "You called me to say you weren't coming, and then left your phone here…so you wouldn't be tempted to answer if I tried to call back."

In her peripheral vision, she saw a man walk to a cabinet. She glanced at him, expecting to tell Andy good-bye. Instantly her mind froze, struggling to accept what she saw.

Daniel?

He got a mug down and poured himself a cup of coffee. When he faced her, he gave her an undeniable smirk.

"Sadie." He nodded once as if her presence here was not the least bit surprising.

She looked at Levi for an explanation. As she stood there, feathery pieces of understanding fell from the clouds surrounding his call yesterday. "How long have you known Daniel?"

Daniel lifted his cup slightly, as if mimicking cheers to her. "A lot longer than he's known you."

Levi pointed toward Daniel. "You stay out of this!"

Sadie focused on Levi. "So this is who you really are, a friend to *him*? And you've chosen to believe whatever he's said, haven't you?" Tears welled. "I will not defend myself." Her heart pounded so hard she felt lightheaded. "But you know me, Levi, better than anyone ever has. Even if that wasn't true, how can you understand animals so very well, but you can't read what's happening here?"

Levi looked at Daniel and then to her. "I understand enough."

"You poor, stupid man."

Levi flinched as if she'd slapped him. "Good-bye, Sadie."

Nineteen

Jonah raised the blinds all the way to the top before taking a step back. "Can you see outside well enough now?"

Beth sat in bed, propped up by numerous fluffy pillows as she eyed his handiwork. "Almost."

Seeing her here, safe and smiling, brought a catch to his throat. He was so happy she was all right, he wouldn't care if she wanted him to re-arrange the bedroom ten more times. Twenty. However many.

The midwife, Mandy, said that Beth had only been having Braxton Hicks and that the baby's huge flop was the positioning of the head in the birthing position—all of which were normal and good things. Even so, Beth's blood pressure and heart rate remained high. So Beth was on bed rest for a few days, just to be safe.

Jonah went to her side, looking out the window from her angle. He shifted the bed a few inches. "How about this?"

"Perfect."

"Gut." He winked, taking the blood pressure cuff off the dresser and sitting on the edge of the bed.

She frowned. "Again?"

Jonah put his index finger over his lips before wrapping the band around her arm and pressing the bulb, watching the digital numbers that blinked her heart rate and blood pressure. The machine beeped time and again before it finally gave a long beep. He read the display, then grinned and removed the cuff. "It's normal."

He put the blood pressure machine on the bed beside her. Was she ready to hear his plan concerning the store and the rest of her pregnancy? He'd been waiting, not wanting to add any stress to the situation. "Listen, sweetheart." He fidgeted with the blankets. "The busyness of the store at Christmastime is enough to make anyone's blood pressure go up. It's only twelve more business days until Christmas. Maybe you should stay out of the store."

Her face clouded, and tears welled, but she nodded, confirming what he'd already suspected: yesterday's event had frightened her as much as it had him. "I don't know if it's necessary to be this careful, but I won't take any chances."

He kissed her forehead. "I love you."

She pursed her lips, wiping tears before she cleared her throat. "You'll need to hire some more workers."

"About a hundred to make up for you not being there." He winked. "Or a few well-trained ones who are familiar with how the store is run." He brushed a wisp of hair from her face. "I've been working on that. I left a message yesterday for Levi to see me today, and he came while you were sleeping. He's agreed to work as needed between now and when the baby is born." He lifted her hand to his lips and kissed it. "I've talked to Lizzy, and she'll work more and not leave town with Omar until after the baby is born. I think that'll get us through."

"I'd always heard it takes a village to raise a child, but I didn't know it took one to get a woman through a pregnancy."

From a love seat in Mammi Lee's sitting room, Sadie watched the snow fall outside the window. Night began to hinder her view as darkness crowded out the day. Her eyes burned from hours of crying, but she now had no more tears to shed.

At least she had all the funds for the mission trip. A trip that could not come soon enough.

Mammi's floor creaked as she entered the room. She had a cup in her hand and held it out to Sadie.

"Denki." Sadie took it, breathing in the aroma of hot apple cider.

"You've been in here for hours, child. Do you want to talk about it?"

Sadie wasn't sure, but she patted the cushion beside her.

Mammi sat beside her and took her hand. "What happened?"

Her throat constricted, and she took several sips of her drink. "I'm sorry, Mammi." She took a deep breath. "I've been lying to you and everyone. I guess I got what I deserved today. If I hadn't been willing to deceive everyone around me, Levi wouldn't be so quick to think me a liar."

"What have you lied about?"

Sadie explained about pretending to court Levi and how she'd fallen in love with him. "Last Sunday, on our way home from an evening with Beth and Jonah, Levi asked me to take this week to think about where I wanted our relationship to go. He said we should stop lying to ourselves, no more hiding from each other behind our walls of pretense." She took a sip of her cider before setting it on an end table. "We were supposed to talk about it last night. But after he didn't arrive when he should've, I went to the phone shanty and got the messages and learned he wasn't coming. That's why I went to see him this morning. For answers."

Mammi pursed her lips. "I told you not to go there this morning. A girl shouldn't be traipsing—"

Sadie jumped up, her hands balled into tight fists. "Why does it always have to be *me* who's wrong?"

Mammi stared at her, mouth slightly agape.

Sadie moved to the window. It'd stopped snowing, and a thin blanket of white covered the yard and fields. "I did everything you and Mamm and Daed and the church leaders asked of me, from the time I began courting Daniel to the day before we were to wed. You know that's true."

Mammi nodded. "I remember it as you've said."

"I put great effort into dotting every *i* and crossing every *t*, but when I saw him with Aquilla, it broke more than my faith in him and my heart. It shattered *me*."

Now Levi had smashed her heart, and all she could do was long for the day she'd leave for Peru—but this time that thought caused an odd sensation inside her. She went to the end table and lifted her drink before sitting on the edge of the chair. The cider was now tepid, but she drank it, trying to examine her motives for taking—and enjoying—her mission trips.

What was it Levi said to her the day they began their pretend courtship? Oh, ya—*I'm beginning to doubt the purity of your motives about mission work. Maybe you just don't want to cope with your parents' expectations.*

Clearly she'd given him more cause to doubt her ability to be honest than she could admit to.

Was she going to Peru to minister to others or to hide from herself? She'd been a nineteen-year-old child when Daniel broke her heart. She'd believed his value as a person was far above hers. She'd thought that by marrying him she'd become more valuable. When he humiliated her, she'd found a way to hide.

Mission work was a worthy goal, and she had no right to use it to

hide from disgrace. Truth was, she'd landed herself in an even more mortifying situation.

"There is no hiding, is there?" She asked herself the question, but then she looked to Mammi. "I mean, what are the chances that all these years later I'd have to face Daniel again?"

"Daniel's a part of your trouble with Levi?" Mammi went to the rocker and sat, staring at Sadie. "You've got to be mistaken, Sadie."

Her words were like a razor that opened an old wound. "Are you ever going to believe me about what I saw that day?"

"It was a confusing mess, and you were so young and impressionable." Mammi stared at the floor, her eyes filling with tears. "I believe you now."

Although her words had a little salve to them, Sadie had already weathered too much at the hands of Daniel's lies for Mammi's response to mean a lot.

"Daed never doubted me." For the first time in years, Sadie longed to talk to him, to soak in his wisdom, maybe even yield to it. "He was good to let me go when I needed to. It had to be hard to set me free as he did—a brokenhearted kid. I love him for it, but all we've done for years is battle each other."

"He's no more perfect in his ways than you or I. But this I do know: he tries so hard where you're concerned."

Sadie saw that now, and she knew what she had to do. She stood.

"I want to go home, Mammi. I need time to talk to Daed before I make any other decisions."

Twenty

*F*or the second time in his life, Levi could not believe he'd treated Sadie so horribly. What kind of a man was he?

"Uncle Levi?"

Even if she were guilty of doing what Daniel had accused her of, she deserved so much more from Levi than he'd given. He should have offered her grace and compassion. He should have been her friend.

But, no, he'd judged her and let Daniel watch as she came undone. He didn't know why Daniel's being here ate at him so much. But it did.

If he went to Mammi Lee's, would she even speak to him?

Tobias slapped the kitchen table. "Uncle Levi!"

Levi glanced up. "What?"

"I've been talking, and you aren't listening." Tobias pointed at Levi's plate. "I thought me and Daed fixed 'em real good. You don't like scrambled eggs anymore?"

"Ya, I like them." He tousled Tobias's hair and forked some eggs. "Hmm, these are the best ever." Then he about choked trying to swallow them. The eggs were fine. They were exactly how he liked them. The same as how he liked life: easy and predictable. "I'm sorry. I'm just not hungry."

"Again?" Tobias scrunched his face and moved in close. "You sick?"

Levi looked to his brother. "Can you call off the dogs?"

"We don't have dogs, Uncle Levi. Only horses." Tobias sprinkled salt on Levi's eggs. "Just how sick are you feeling today?"

Andy removed the plate from in front of Levi. "Tobias, finish getting ready for school."

Tobias skipped out of the room and began singing about puppies.

"He's right about one thing." Andy swiped bits of egg off the table. "You gotta start eating."

It'd been three days since Levi had seen Sadie. Three days of not eating or sleeping. Three days without a minute of peace. He kept expecting his mind to stop going over things at some point and give him a break. But it hadn't happened yet.

Andy put the dishes in the sink. "You at the store today, your workshop, or training horses?"

Levi couldn't take it anymore. He had to talk about what ate at him before he lost his mind. "Why'd she leave?"

"Sadie?"

"Eva."

Andy scratched his head. "You know, seeing as it was me who lost a wife, you sure do carry a lot of scars."

"She was family. Like you and Tobias. But she just walked out. Who does that? And why?"

Andy poured coffee into a mug and sat across from Levi. "I know we should've talked about this a long time ago, but I couldn't." He swiped his hand across the table. "You and I are better suited for working and arguing, even for building a home worthy of raising Tobias. But we're not good at talking about the hard things."

"I can't deny that."

Andy rapped his fingers on the table. "But you needed me to talk, and I'm sorry I didn't. Eva was...a sinking ship. She didn't have the emotional strength to get through a day on her own. If you look back, you can see that. She stayed in bed most of the day, and when she got up, she needed help to do the simplest chores. Even at sixteen, I saw hints of that in her, but I didn't have to see it, because she told me about her struggles. She was completely overwhelmed by life, and despite knowing better, I chose to lie to myself, chose to believe that I had it in me to keep her afloat."

Levi remembered wondering why Eva had no zing to her, no desire to greet the day and enjoy it for what it was. He also struggled to understand why she'd make such a big deal out of the smallest things sometimes. But Levi had accepted Eva as she came. And now he couldn't accept any woman for who she was. He made himself sick.

Andy took a sip of his coffee. "I think Sadie is exactly who she told you she was from the start—no angel. But think about that night she helped you, and open your eyes—she's not Eva. She's strong and able to see a challenge through." He chuckled. "And she may always be in hot water with her Daed, but her joy for life is contagious."

Dozens of memories washed over Levi. "She's got this unreasonable fear of rodents, but that never stops her from doing what she sets out to do. It's one of my favorite things about her." Levi rubbed the back of his neck, grateful he no longer needed the neck brace. "None of what you've said helps me understand how Eva could've left Tobias."

Andy looked down the hall, checking for Tobias before he leaned in. "After he was born, she was more overwhelmed. Eva didn't believe she'd be a decent mother, and the idea of failing him—of having more babies—terrified her." Andy sighed. "Look, I know I sort of went crazy when she left, and I leaned on you too much. But this is a good life, and I have peace about the decisions I made that got me here. You've got to find some peace, Levi. You've got to learn to trust that if you ever have to face the unthinkable, God will be right there to give you strength. And so will I."

"Me too." Tobias walked into the room, smiling.

Levi glanced at Andy, and his eyes grew wide before he shrugged. Had Tobias heard much of what Andy had said or only the ending? But he knew by Andy's reaction that if Tobias had heard, he was okay with it.

"So who's taking me to school, because I don't want to walk. It's too cold out there!"

"I'll take you." Levi got up. "And then I'm going to apologize to Sadie. But that's all I can do."

Andy stared at him, looking as if he felt sorry for him. But Levi knew what he knew. Despite having strength and joy, she'd left Daniel the same as Eva had left Andy.

And he couldn't ignore that.

It didn't take long for Levi to hitch up the carriage and drop Tobias at school. Soon he stood on Mammi Lee's porch, as nervous as a mistreated horse. He lifted a hand and knocked on the door.

Someone moved the curtains back from the glass and peered out. A moment later Mammi Lee opened the door.

"Hi, Verna. I...need to speak to Sadie."

Mammi Lee stepped back from the door, and he came inside. "She's not here. Left a couple of days ago."

Levi knew it wasn't time for her to leave, not yet. Had she already gone ahead to be with some of her team? "But she's still in the States, right?"

She walked into the living room.

He followed her. "Do you know how I can reach her?"

Mammi pulled another towel from the pile. "Why do you want to talk to her?"

"I need to apologize. I…I wasn't much of a friend."

"So it's *friends* you want to be." She popped the towel in the air. "Is that the conclusion you came to during that week of thinking before you and she were supposed to talk—that you just want to be *friends*?"

"Mammi Lee…Verna, I—"

"That's a yes-or-no question, Levi."

He closed his eyes, seeing the only thing he'd seen for months: Sadie. "What do you want from me? You want the truth? I love her. How could any man get to know her like I have and not fall in love with her? But it's never going to work between us. We both knew that from the start. Still, I need to talk to her."

"Is that what you were going to tell her last Saturday night—that it'd never work? Or did Daniel change your mind for you?" She set the folded towel on top of the others.

Her question didn't leave him anywhere to hide. And he finally saw. That's what he'd been doing, wasn't it? Hiding. Sadie had spent years pulling away from her family to hide—whether in Stone Creek or Peru. And he hid while living right here among his family and looking them in the eye every day.

Mammi Lee walked toward the door. "It's time you leave now."

"But—"

"You can rest your worry. Sadie will be fine. She'll grieve for a while, and then she'll be stronger and happier without you, just like she's been without Daniel. You're making the same mistake I did—you believe Daniel's lies. And just like me, you'll see the truth one day. And you'll be sorry for trusting the wrong person, but it won't matter to her by then."

Did he really believe Daniel, or did he simply *want* to believe him?

Verna opened the door. "We've been praying for her night and day for years, hoping she'd land right where she is."

There was only one place her family had been praying for her to be. "She's in Brim."

"I'll be sure she knows you came by, and I'll say that you'd like to remain friends and you're sorry, but I think it'd be best if you leave it at that. Please."

He stepped onto the porch, and she closed the door. Verna had freed him, had made it clear Sadie would be fine. Her reasoning deserved his respect. He should do as she asked and not try to reach Sadie.

So if he was free, why did he hurt worse now than before?

He drove his rig toward home. Dozens of emotions gnawed at him. It didn't matter what had taken place between Daniel and Sadie, did it? The problem was *him*.

His inability to let himself really care, to trust his heart to someone other than himself.

Still…

Levi's back teeth clenched. What *had* happened with Sadie and Daniel? He wanted to know the truth. He pulled his phone out of his pocket and called Daniel.

"Levi, where are you? I'm at your place, arguing with Andy about taking a horse. You know how he gets."

When Levi topped the hill near his home, he spotted the horse trailer. He hung up and drove onto his driveway.

Andy had Lightning, a white filly, by the harness, standing at the back of the open trailer. He and Daniel had talked about this. No horse would be sold until Levi said it was ready.

Levi got out of his rig and strode toward the trailer. Tip sat in the truck as usual.

Daniel spat a wad of gum onto the ground. "We've got a buyer willing to pay top price for this filly so she can be a Christmas present."

"She's not ready."

"Well, she may not be perfectly trained, but you've been working with her."

"She goes nowhere." Levi turned to Andy. "Take her back to the barn."

Andy patted Lightning and hurried the animal toward the barn.

"Why?" Daniel's voice echoed off the barn. "Buyers know the risks of owning an animal like this. Our goal has always been to make the horses reasonably obedient and move on to the next sale."

Levi could hardly absorb seeing Daniel in this light. He was wound tighter than Levi had ever seen him. Maybe it bothered him that Sadie had learned to care for someone else. But did his business partner realize he'd just lied? Their goal was never as Daniel just said. But everyone tends to get rather gray about things as time passes.

"Our agreement was never casual or careless when it came to selling horses. And I've made my sentiments about training them clear."

Daniel sighed. "Okay." He put up both hands. "I didn't come here for a fight. I assumed you'd be ready to let her go and make some good money. What about Amigo? Any chance he's ready? I'm sure you've done your magic by now. He's bound to be as rehabilitated as he'll ever get."

"None of the horses are ready. You took the last of the trained ones just four days ago."

"Well, sometimes you get a lot done in a few days. I bet you got one that'll work to fill this order."

That was nothing but flattery. Levi couldn't get to know any horse well within a few days, even if the horse already had some training. Levi needed repeat performances to ensure a behavior was ingrained.

"You're just a smooth talker, aren't you, Daniel?"

Daniel kicked at the gravel, moving his foot back and forth while clearing a spot. "This argument isn't about the filly or Amigo, is it? It's about Sadie, right? You came here ready to fight."

Daniel had some good points. Levi had climbed out of his rig thinking about Sadie and suspecting Daniel. But Daniel's earlier use of the word *rehabilitate* had caught Levi's attention. They didn't refer to horses in that manner unless something had happened to the animal that it needed to recover from—mistreatment, an accident, illness.

Levi's mind churned, burning through dozens of past conversations. Andy returned, and Levi looked to him. "Daniel just said something about Amigo needing to be rehabilitated. Do you recall anything about that in any discussion or seeing it in the paperwork when he unloaded Amigo here last spring?"

"No. I'd have remembered if it'd been said or listed anywhere."

Levi didn't doubt that Andy would've paid heed to it. His brother pored over the information that came in, often calling previous owners and taking careful notes on each horse. He shared that information with Levi at great length before Levi began working with them.

"Oh, come on!" Daniel's face turned red. "There is no way I'd do anything on purpose that would get you hurt. You've got to know that much. We're friends. Besides, what would be the point? I need you to be whole if I'm going to make the kind of money we do when working as a team."

"So you messed up and didn't provide that information to me. Is that what you're saying?"

"Ya, absolutely. It was a mistake. I don't know how I could forget that Amigo had been traumatized by some boys playing with firecrackers. He got tangled up in some wire fencing running away from them. You needed to know that. But I didn't recall it until after you were hurt. What good would it have done after you were injured to tell you I had messed up?"

Levi stared at him. He believed Daniel's account of overlooking crucial information where Amigo was concerned. But he was beginning to realize that this man was very good at covering up his mistakes.

In that moment Levi saw the truth. He didn't know why, but he could clearly see that Sadie had good cause to call off the wedding, just as she'd had good cause to go riding the night she'd found Levi in that field: God had directed her steps.

That revelation, however, brought him no relief or peace. Daniel had lied to him—more than once. And Levi had swallowed it. And Sadie had been hurt.

Levi had given up his chance with her because he'd believed a lie, not just the one Daniel told, but the one he'd told himself: that he had insight into how much of a gamble it was to get involved with a woman. But that wasn't insight. That was fear, and he'd chosen to believe it because he'd thought it would keep him safe and far away from a deceitful heart. And yet here he stood.

Daniel shoved his hands into his coat pockets, his shoulders stooped. "I'm sorry, Levi. You've got to believe me. It was a stupid mistake not to tell you about Amigo. Please give me a chance to make it up to you."

"I believe you. It's not like you to do something deceitful on purpose, any more than it was when you cheated on Sadie. Right?"

"Sadie?" Daniel rolled his eyes. "Is every conversation from here on going to circle back to her?"

"I'm in love with her. Can you understand that?"

"Far more than you'll ever give me credit for." Daniel sighed. "Okay."

Daniel's last word seemed to lodge in his throat, and an unfamiliar expression eased across his face. Was he going to be honest?

"I'm not like you, Levi. Never was. I've spent most of my life being so restless I can't stand myself. I've given into temptation more times than

I'm willing to admit. But when I got to know Sadie, I knew she was my best chance of finding peace and happiness. I'd hoped to be a good husband. But her cousin was *so* beautiful. And we were both smitten. I wanted to resist. I just…couldn't."

"You've lied about what happened since the day she caught you. When I told you I loved her, you lied to me. That's very deliberate."

"I had to lie. If the church leaders had known what happened, I would've been shunned. My family would've…"

"What, seen you for who you are?"

"I was so angry that she wouldn't give me another chance. But I never meant for any of this to happen. I'll make it up to you…and Sadie."

"No. We're done." He gestured toward the truck. "Just go."

"But we make great money with our horse-trading. We need to work through this. I told you the truth. That's gotta count for something."

Levi stepped forward, his hands balling into fists. "You and I are done. I'm not doing any more business with you, and if you think that's unfair,"—he met Daniel's stunned gaze—"feel free to take it up with God. He knows *exactly* how to handle someone who isn't just."

Twenty-One

*A*n icy wind rattled the windows and howled as Sadie set the dinner table. Each move she made inside her childhood homestead was as familiar as a Pennsylvania winter and yet as foreign as if she'd never lived here. A fire crackled in the hearth.

She'd come home. She'd yielded to her Daed's authority, and he'd embraced her with tears flowing. He didn't want her to leave the country again, and she'd called the head of the mission team and told him she wouldn't be going. The mission director understood that these things happen, and they had a young man who wanted to go. He could take her place, but he lacked the necessary funds. She became his sponsor and sent all her money to the board. It hadn't been easy, but she'd done as she thought God wanted—and she had peace.

Still, her heart ached, and she missed things about Levi she hadn't been consciously aware of, like the steady calmness of his movements as he worked with a piece of wood or his quiet tone when they talked. He had a zeal for life, and even his cynicism drew her in, as he never used it meanly. How many times had she startled awake because she saw him in her dreams, saw his smile from across the room when they went to singings, felt his sorrow, heard him calling to her?

Tomorrow was Christmas Eve, and she kept telling herself that the ache would pass after the holidays.

If only she could believe that.

The back door opened, and a rush of cold air came in with her father. "Sadie?"

"I'm right here."

He glanced at the kitchen table. "Yes, you are." He pulled off his coat. "I just got off the phone with Mammi Lee. I think we should talk."

Emotions flooded through her, and tears pricked her eyes. "Is it about Levi?"

"It is." He went to his chair beside the fireplace. Sadie went to the ladder back that faced the hearth. Her mother sat in the love seat across from her husband. Daed smiled, but his eyes looked sad. "It's not the first time since you arrived home last week that I've spoken with her. We thought it best not to be hasty. Levi came to her place more than a week ago, looking for you, and Mammi Lee asked him not to contact you."

Sadie waited, hardly able to keep her poise.

"A few days after Levi's visit, his brother came to see her. He didn't want to interfere, but he wanted her to know something that'd happened—in case she wanted to share it with you."

"Daed!" Sadie reached over and swatted his knee. "You're dragging this out too long. Tell me."

"It didn't take your Levi very long to come to his senses. He broke off all ties with Daniel."

Her heart jolted, and she wasn't sure how to feel about that piece of news. Did it mean Levi finally saw Daniel's true character and would no longer associate with him, or was it something more? Did he care for her so much that he had to do something drastic to heal some of the rift between them? "Why?"

"Well, I have it on good authority that he's a fine man who's reluctantly fallen in love with my daughter."

Her heart soared. Was it possible? She prayed it was.

The flames in the fireplace swooshed as a log shifted. And a memory caught her. Years ago she had sat in this same spot, broken beyond words and staring at a cold hearth.

A smile rose from within, and she looked at her mother. "Can we spend Christmas in Apple Ridge?"

Daed rocked back in his chair. "I see no reason why not, as long as we can find a driver on such short notice."

Mamm stood. "I've spent many a year doing favors for Englisch friends—baby-sitting, catering meals, and such. I know people who'll want to help. Maybe one of them will be able to do so, even on Christmas Eve."

❦

Energy surged through Beth's body as she basted a ham. With so much time lately to devote to everyday chores—washing clothes and hanging them out, sewing new outfits for herself and Jonah and the baby, quilting, baking, making Christmas cards—she'd thought she had liveliness to spare. Today a stronger wave of desire to cook and clean and organize flooded her.

Of course, her good-natured husband remained by her side, making sure she didn't overdo anything. Jonah mashed the sweet potatoes, shoving the utensil into the pot of orange pulp again and again. "This seems like a lot of food for two people."

"Look at the upside. We won't need to cook for days."

"I sort of thought the idea of a quiet celebration was for you to stay off your feet."

"And I will. As soon as we celebrate today with a feast."

Suddenly a wave of Braxton Hicks hit her as she pushed the rack into the oven. Her lower back stung, and her thighs ached as the contraction grew stronger.

"Well, whatever we do, it'll be easier and safer than going out in this weather tonight. I certainly don't want you doing all it'd take to have that monstrous crowd known as your family coming here for their festivities." Jonah knocked the potato masher against the rim of the pan. "Smooth enough?"

Beth evened her breathing, surprised by the force of the contraction. "Ya…it looks good to me."

But rather than fading like usual, the contraction grew stronger. She clutched the counter, waiting for it to subside. The midwife had said she'd already dilated to a three but that women often stayed that way until their due date. Right now, Beth didn't know what to think.

"Sweetheart?" Jonah moved to her side.

"If that was a Braxton Hicks, it carried some real force."

"When was the last one?"

"Ten minutes ago. Until an hour ago I hadn't had any in days." Beth fumbled with her apron, trying to reach inside the hidden pocket. It was time to use the cell phone her midwife gave her. "I think I'll give Mandy a call to see what she thinks."

She planned to sound calm, but the idea of going into labor four weeks early made her feel sick, and she prayed for God's protection over her child.

Snow fell harder and harder as Levi ushered the last employees out the door at Hertzlers'. It was time they all went home. There was no sense in letting snow accumulate and risk someone's having a difficult time getting home on Christmas Eve. He could handle the rest of today by himself, even if customers might have to wait until he could get to them.

Mattie was still here, however. She had customers picking up Christmas cakes, and Levi couldn't run the register, fetch layaways, and run the counter for Mattie Cakes.

The next few hours at the store weren't too busy, and as the snow deepened, people stopped coming in.

He stepped onto the porch and watched the white flakes silently fall from the black sky. The air smelled of Christmas, and everyone he'd come into contact with lately seemed to be in a festive mood, especially Tobias. But it didn't feel like a joyous holiday to Levi. What was Sadie doing today? Did she miss him? Would she miss him when she was in Peru?

As hard as he'd tried, he couldn't stop thinking about her. But he'd finally accepted the truth: it was his lot from now on to miss her. He went back into the store.

With the store empty, he went to the Mattie Cakes nook to see what was happening in her little area of the store. Mattie sat at a small table, talking to her husband.

Levi smiled. "Hey, Gideon. I didn't see you come in."

Gideon stood and said, "Merry Christmas, Levi."

"Denki. Same to you."

Gideon took a seat. "We're waiting on one more customer to pick up a cake, and then I'm taking Mattie home, where she can open the birthday presents her family has been dropping off throughout the day."

"Oh, that's right. I forgot. Happy birthday, Mattie."

"Denki, Levi."

"Gideon, take her and get out. When that customer shows up, I'll be here."

Gideon leaned in and kissed his wife. "What do you say, Mattie Lane? May I take you home?"

"Absolutely. We've got some singing to do along the way."

Gideon laughed. "We married folks can't go to any more Christmas singings. We need to have a private session, and it just happens to be the perfect weather for a sleigh ride."

Mattie grinned. "We're borrowing Beth and Jonah's sleigh?"

Gideon helped her get on her coat. "I worked it out with him before coming in today. Beth and Jonah send their birthday and Christmas wishes too."

Mattie kissed his cheek. "This sleigh ride isn't all you have planned, is it?"

"I'm not telling—not yet." Gideon winked at Levi.

Mattie put on her black winter bonnet. "The cake should've been picked up an hour ago. If June Smith doesn't arrive in another hour, she isn't coming."

"Okay."

Mattie waved at him as she left. "Merry Christmas, Levi."

"Merry Christmas." He closed the door behind them. The ticking of the clocks that lined the walls echoed through the quiet store.

He grabbed a push broom and began going down the aisles. He straightened shelves and returned items from the register area to their spot. No one else came in, and he finally put the Closed sign in the window.

"Welcome to your future, Levi," he mumbled. He'd wanted to live out his days as a bachelor, and he'd managed to give himself exactly that. *What a great gift idea. You should be proud.*

Before Sadie, he hadn't felt lonely, let alone miserable. What had she done to him—stretched his tiny heart until it could hold the vastness of his love for her? Now he had a huge heart and nothing to fill it.

He went through the store turning off the gas lamps. Since he'd ridden here bareback, he'd take the cake the customer never picked up to Beth and Jonah, wish them a Merry Christmas, and head home.

He emptied the register and took the cash to the safe in Beth's office. The bells on the door rang, and he went in that direction. It had to be Jonah.

Standing just inside the doorway, he saw the shadowy figure of an Amish woman in a winter coat and hat.

"You're just in time, Mrs. Smith. The cake is right over here."

She turned.

"Sadie!" His heart beat faster, and he nearly ran to her.

She shivered all over, and he grabbed a quilt from the display rack and wrapped it around her. He rubbed her arms through the layers of thickness, trying to warm her.

"What are you doing here?"

She shook. "I've been in Apple Ridge for hours, even spent some time with Andy and Tobias, waiting for you to get home. Then it struck me to come here so we could talk privately. Andy wasn't a fan of the idea, but I wouldn't listen to him." She drew a shaky breath. "Horses and buggies are better at getting around in the snow than cars and trucks, right?"

"Ya. I've used a horse and carriage to pull more than one four-wheeler out of a ditch."

She rubbed her gloved hands together. "Then why'd I have such a hard time getting here?"

"The roads must be bad, and you shouldn't have been on them."

"Like I shouldn't have been out riding the night I found you on the ground?"

"This is different, Sadie." He tugged at the fingertips of her gloves until he slid the half-frozen knit things right off. "You were in no danger that night." He sandwiched her cold hands between his, warming them.

"Actually." She shivered. "As things turned out, that's arguable."

"I suppose it is." If he could undo any of his rash behavior, he would. He kissed her hands before covering them again with his own. Would she think that too forward? Was she here to let him know they could remain friends like they'd agreed to be when they began their pretend courtship? He didn't want to do any more damage to their relationship—it was Christmas Eve, and she was here. That was far more than he'd dared to hope for. Still, he couldn't throttle his foolish heart.

He led her to Mattie Cakes and held a chair for her.

Although he didn't want to leave her side, he went to put a kettle of water on the stove and struck a match to light the burner. He could fix either tea or hot chocolate faster than he could fix a pot of coffee, and she needed something hot as soon as he could get it ready. "Tea?" He held up a box of peppermint tea bags. "Or hot chocolate?"

"Hot chocolate, please." She folded her hands on the table.

As he opened a pouch of powdery chocolate mix and dumped it into a mug, she said, "Levi, I think I know what happened the Saturday night we were supposed to talk. I'd like to know if it's accurate."

A shudder ran through him. *Please, God.* "Okay."

"The feelings you have for me are like a skittish and unfamiliar horse. Daniel was like the booming fireworks. And 'the horse' threw you. You landed hard and were too addled to think clearly."

He liked her analogy. It was very Sadie-like—honest but kind. He poured hot water into the mug and stirred. "I'm sorry." He set the mug in front of her and took a seat.

She wrapped her hands around it. "So Mammi Lee said." She took a sip. "The thing is, we have unfinished business. And while we're here where we can talk openly and freely, I want to know what you had planned to say that Saturday night before Daniel showed up."

He went to the display case and took out the cake the customer hadn't picked up. He removed it from its box and set it on the table between them. "It'll take a while to explain it all."

She peered at the many colors of the frosting. "It's beautiful."

He passed her a fork, kept one for himself, and sat down. "Mattie's cakes taste even better than they look. Dive in."

They ate several bites and shared the cup of cocoa.

Sadie peeled out of the blanket and her coat. "I about froze to death to get here to talk to you. You can't keep stalling."

He forked a bite of cake. "Try me."

She raised an eyebrow. "You want to eat the cake or wear it?"

He chuckled. "Okay. What I wanted to say was—"

Bells jangled. "Levi?"

At Jonah's yell, Levi stood. "Over here."

Jonah motioned for him as he made his way to the office. "We need to reach the midwife. We've called her twice, and each time she gave us some instructions. Now it seems her phone's not working." Jonah picked up the phone, punched several numbers, and waited. "Same as what's happening with the cell she gave Beth. We can't get through. It goes straight to voice mail, but it won't let me leave a message."

Sadie came up behind Levi. "Is she in labor?"

"The midwife didn't think so, but Beth's water broke ten minutes ago. I can't take her out in this weather. An ambulance can't get through, either—at least, not until morning. The baby will be premature, not by a lot, but we have to get Mandy here. She's been delivering babies for forever. She'll know what to do with a preemie."

"Where does she live?"

"Barton's Ridge."

Levi let out a whistle. "Even if you reach her, chances are she can't get here on her own."

Jonah pressed his fingers into his forehead and closed his eyes. "I know nothing about these things. Lizzy would at least know something about delivering a baby, and I've tried to reach her, but she and Omar are at his children's place for the evening. Obviously no one can hear the phone ringing in the shanty."

Sadie moved closer to the desk. "I'm not your best bet, but I have helped with several births. One was premature, and I watched a midwife tend to her."

"That helps, Sadie. Thanks. If you two will stay with Beth, I'll go on horseback."

Levi stepped forward. "I'll go. Beth needs you."

Jonah studied him. "It's bad out there. And Barton's Ridge is dangerous any time of year."

"I'll get through."

Twenty-Two

*S*adie paced the floors, stopping every few minutes to look out the window in the dark of night. No sign of anyone. It'd been hours, and they'd heard nothing. At least a dozen times she'd checked the cell phone the midwife gave Beth, but was it even getting a signal? She and Jonah were taking turns sitting with Beth.

Jonah came to the doorway, looking as if he were the one in pain. One look told him all he needed to know. No one had arrived. He left the bedroom door ajar. "She's dozing."

Sadie poured him a cup of coffee. "She'll be fine, and so will the little one."

Jonah nodded before taking a sip, but he didn't look convinced. "I haven't told you that it's nice to see you back in Apple Ridge. Will you be staying long?"

"I hope so."

"Has anyone told you the story of Beth and me?"

"No."

They heard Beth moan long and loud. Coffee spilled from Jonah's cup as he set it down. They both hurried to the bedroom.

Beth clutched each side of the pillow behind her head and panted. When the contraction eased, Jonah held her hand. "Sadie doesn't know our story."

Beth smiled. "I'd like to hear it too."

"One hot summer day I was minding my own business. I was in Pete's Antiques in Ohio, and this beautiful young woman about ran over me in her all-business-all-the-time way." Jonah told of the many months of letter writing and getting to know each other and the inevitable discovery of secrets that threatened to end their friendship. He stopped talking each time Beth had a contraction.

"Then, on a Christmas Eve night much like this one, Beth tried to get from Pennsylvania to Ohio to let me know she loved me and would marry me."

"Really?" Sadie sat on the edge of her chair. "That's what I'm doing here...sort of. Only I'm not sure how Levi feels."

Beth and Jonah gave each other a look. Beth smiled. "Be bold, Sadie." She groaned the words before she gasped and gripped Jonah's hands as another contraction took command of her body.

An odd rumbling sound vibrated the room. Jonah glanced at Sadie, and she left the bedroom to hurry down the hallway and onto the front porch. Lights shone in her eyes from an odd-looking vehicle coming straight toward her. A minute later the vehicle turned, and she saw a huge green tractor with an enclosed cab. An Amish woman with a medical bag climbed down. "Has she delivered?"

"Not yet." Sadie peered into the cab, desperate to see Levi. But all she saw was an Englisch man.

"Help him get the incubator and the car battery into the house."

"Where's Levi?"

She paused. "I don't know. On his way to find me, he saw a couple stranded in a ditch. He went back to help them while I finished delivering another baby. It was a long labor, but Levi never showed."

She placed her hand on Sadie's shoulder. "I'm sure he's fine."

But Sadie had heard Jonah's description. She imagined sheer drop-offs that couldn't be easily spotted on a clear day, let alone at night. In weather like this, a treacherous ridge could swallow lives whole.

Mandy grasped her arm. "Go on. Help Parker. He'll be wantin' to get back home as soon as he can."

Sadie stayed busy doing everything Mandy asked, but she'd never prayed so fervently in her life—for safety for Beth, her baby, and Levi. When Mandy no longer needed her for a bit, she hurried across the parking lot to the store and used the office phone to call Levi's cell. It went to voice mail. His phone apparently wasn't charged—again. She battled thoughts of his lying somewhere in the freezing snow. The moment she stepped back into Beth and Jonah's home, she heard Mandy.

"Kumm, Beth, push," Mandy coaxed. "It won't be much longer. Push."

Beth moaned, long and hard, and then—

A baby wailed.

Joy rose within Sadie.

Then silence.

Sadie waited, her heart pounding. She moved down the hallway and listened outside the closed door. She heard soft voices talking and Beth crying.

Sadie's eyes filled with tears. *Dear God, please.*

Should she go in?

She leaned her head against the doorframe and prayed. The door creaked open, and Jonah stood there, his eyes filled with tears. He smiled. "I have a healthy son and a strong, beautiful wife." He laughed and wiped his cheeks. "Kumm."

She stepped into the room.

Mandy was grinning. "That little one weighs a good six and a half pounds. He's technically a preemie, so keep a watch on his breathing, but he's a healthy boy if I've ever seen one. Pink as anything."

Beth continued to cry. "Look." She shifted the bundle in her arms up just a bit for Sadie to see him better.

Sadie edged in closer. "Merry Christmas."

Another round of sobs broke from Beth, and she looked to Jonah. "Merry Christmas, sweetheart."

Jonah moved to her side and brushed some damp hair from Beth's face. "Merry Christmas, indeed."

Sadie and Mandy slipped out of the room.

It wasn't long before everyone except Sadie was dozing. She pulled an armchair in front of the window. The snow clouds were gone, and the stars shone bright, but she saw no evidence of a moon. *Dear God, please help Levi get home safely.*

She studied the dark, white landscape until the sky wasn't quite as dark as before. In the distance she saw something moving, maybe a deer. She studied it for a moment, then rose to her feet to get a closer look.

Levi?

She slid into her shoes and grabbed her coat. She hurried through the house on her tiptoes. Once on the porch, she saw a man in snowshoes taking one slow step at a time.

"Levi!"

She ran as fast as she could through the white blanket. He spotted her and removed his snowshoes. As soon as he stood, she careened into his arms, knocking him over. They both tumbled into the snow, but she didn't care.

"Are you okay?"

"Before or after this encounter?"

She laughed, caressing his face. "I was so worried."

"I know." He gazed into her eyes. "I've been doing everything I could to get here. I didn't want you to worry. How's Beth?"

"The midwife got here, and Beth and Jonah have a healthy baby boy."

"Gut. Now I've got something I want to say." He pulled a glove off and ran the backs of his fingers against her cheek. "I love you, Sadie. And I want to marry you if you'll have me. If you need to serve a year or two of missions first, I'll wait. But I don't want to live a lifetime without you."

His words burrowed deep into her soul. He loved her! Not only did he want to marry her. He trusted her enough to fearlessly do so. Her heart jumped and skipped, but she couldn't find her voice.

Thank You, God, for bringing Levi and me together, for being greater than all the trials that have damaged and molded us.

Her soul overflowed, but she was unable to respond. She stood, and then helped him up. She picked up the snowshoes and held them up to him, silently asking questions.

He shook his head. "I've had a night like I can't believe. The kind only God could get me through." He put his arm around her shoulders, and they began walking toward the house. "I'd say someone's been praying."

She looked up at him. "Lots of someones—including me. One of my prayers went like this: 'Dear God, please help Levi get home so I can tell him that I'm not leaving Apple Ridge and that I'll make an excellent wife—not perfect, mind you, but excellent.'"

Levi halted and studied her. "Well, I survived last night, and I'm right here with you. I mean...I'm not dreaming."

She smiled. "I could slap you to prove it."

He barked out a laugh. "The first memory I have of you is being slapped, and then you threatened to do it again if I didn't stay awake."

"And look at us now. If something proves successful, it bears repeating. But we've grown a bit since then. Maybe I should kick you instead."

He laughed and pulled her into his arms. Despite his exhaustion, she felt the magnitude of strength within him. As cold as the air around them was, all she could feel was the warmth of his love.

He held her close. "I look forward to a lifetime of being with you. How about a kiss instead?"

"Well...since it is Christmas."

His warm lips met hers and lingered. "Merry Christmas, Sadie."

"The first of many, Levi." And she looked forward to every day with him between each Christmas, to honor and cherish him and their marriage, to assure him there was nowhere she'd rather be than by his side.

She lowered her head to his chest as the beauty of dawn began to sparkle against the snow. The sky held clouds of lavender and pink and orange.

It was a dawn to remember—the first one they'd share—the dawn of their first Christmas.

Oatmeal and Honey Soap

9 ounces olive oil

4 ounces coconut oil

3 ounces palm oil

1 ounce castor oil

$\frac{1}{4}$ cup colloidal oatmeal

1 ounce honey

2.52 ounces lye

8 fluid ounces water

*optional: extra whole oats and honey

Directions:

1. Prepare the lye water. Set it aside to cool.
2. Melt the solid oils together. Set them aside to cool.
3. Mix the olive oil, castor oil, and oatmeal.
4. When the solid oils are approximately 120° Fahrenheit and the lye water has cooled to approximately 100° Fahrenheit, gently pour the lye water into the oils. (Never pour oils into lye.)
5. Stir until trace.*

---

*   Trace is the stage of soap making when the ingredients are fully mixed and ready for additives and pouring into molds. In the mixing process when the ingredients resemble vanilla pudding, when the mixture is thick enough that dripping some of it across the top of the mixture leaves a trail of drips that don't immediately sink back into the liquid, you have reached trace.

6. Add the oatmeal mixture and then the honey until well mixed.
7. Pour into prepared molds and cover with plastic wrap. (Optional: sprinkle whole oats and drizzle honey lightly over the top of the curing soap.)
8. Allow to stand covered for 48 hours.
9. Remove from molds and cut as desired.
10. Allow to age in open air for 2 to 3 weeks before using.

I'd like to thank a reader friend for sharing her soap recipe with us. Thank you, Kristin Lail! I connected with Kristin through Facebook and later discovered she's an avid reader and book reviewer who loves to make soaps. She's a wife and mom to five daughters. If you'd like to read Kristin's reviews or purchase some of her soaps, you'll find her website at www.ASimplyEnchantedLife.com. Or you can find her on Facebook at https://www.facebook.com/Senchanted.